WHY BLACKMAIL?

Anabel was loaded. She owned one of New York's most successful nightclubs, a block of paying apartments in LA, and a beautiful body that was like money in the bank. So why did the stripper suddenly resort to blackmail? Just when she had it made, why did she decide to play such a dangerous game?

A Park Avenue executive hires Peter Chambers to get back some indiscreet letters he wrote to a famous strip-tease artist, and the tough private eye smashes into the most fiendish plot of his career—where blackmail doesn't figure, but murder does.

Henry Kane

My Business Is MURDER

SIGNET BOOKS

A SIGNET BOOK

Published by
The New American Library

First Printing, February, 1965

SIGNET TRADEMARK REG. U.S. PAT. OFF. AND FOREIGN COUNTRIES
REGISTERED TRADEMARK—MARCA REGISTRADA
HECHO EN CHICAGO, U.S.A.

SIGNET BOOKS are published by
The New American Library of World Literature, Inc.
501 Madison Avenue, New York, New York 10022

PRINTED IN THE UNITED STATES OF AMERICA

I

THE BIG TOUCH

CHAPTER 1

Why blackmail?

I intended to ask exactly that question. Tonight.

It didn't fit. And blackmail always figures to fit.

It puzzled me, but it didn't detract from my rapt attention as I watched her take her clothes off. You and I can take our clothes off—we do it every day—and it doesn't mean a thing, one way or another. But with Anabel Jolly it was special. She took her clothes off with grace and spirit, revealing a lush, long-legged, firm-thighed, narrow-waisted, full-bosomed, dazzling whiteness, and she strutted, proudly and defiantly.

Anabel Jolly had made a good thing of taking off her clothes. It was rumored that she had received as high as $5000 per week for the simple operation, if simple is the word, of removing her clothes under a blue light on a small stage before a select and palpitating public. She had worked all the best clubs in the country from Hollywood to New York, and right now she was performing her specialty in a club of her own appropriately, if mildly, entitled Club Jolly.

Then—once more—why blackmail?

Blackmail is old-fashioned, and there was nothing old-fashioned about Anabel Jolly. Blackmail is dangerous—and although Anabel Jolly was as dangerous a female as ever it has been my pleasure to encounter—the danger involved, piquant and exciting and practically overwhelming, was directed *from* Anabel Jolly *at* all comers (provided such comers were male). Futhermore, Anabel Jolly wasn't looking for trouble—not blackmail trouble. She didn't need it. Anabel Jolly was loaded. I had put in ten days of intensive spade work before I had met her. I knew all about her. She didn't have to break the law to obtain money. She had money. She had plenty of money.

So . . . why the blackmail?

I pondered that, sitting alone at a small round table, an appreciative patron at the Club Jolly. The house was packed and attentive and I applauded with the rest of the boobs and I meant it. Anabel Jolly was a peeler, but she was the best in the business and the best is always something. Anabel Jolly was an artist. There are others who have the equipment: structure, beauty, grace and rhythm. Anabel Jolly had more. She combined a display of sex with an air of contempt, a warmth of movement with a frigid poise, a voluptuous wriggling body with a cold and arrogant mein: her eyes were slits that viewed her viewers with disdain: it was as though she erected an invisible barrier between herself and her audience: she was naked but untouchable, and out of reach. And the suckers loved it.

She did her last bump, her last grind, stood stock-still with her arms outflung, her body in a crouch, her eyes wide open now, the smile of contempt on her mouth—and the curtain closed about her. The lights came on and the hub-bub grew and the waiters stalked the tables. This was the last show and most of the patrons paid their checks and departed. I had another drink and waited. I had a date with Anabel Jolly. This was the fifth night running I'd had a date with Anabel Jolly, and I'd enjoyed every one of them, but tonight I was going to put it to her about the blackmail, and that was a prospect I didn't enjoy. I looked down at my watch. It was five to four in the morning.

The tables around me were wearing their chairs when she finally joined me. She rubbed a cool finger along the back of my neck and sid, "Hi, Lover."

Lover grinned upward. "Bar's closed. You can have a sip of mine, if a sip is needful."

"More than one sip is needful, Sweetie. Let's get out of here."

I paid and we went. It was warm out, a warm night in October, Indian summer hanging over the town like an omen of doom. I waved to a cab and we rolled, windows down, toward Harlem to an after-hours' joint called Jackson's. There was dancing in Jackson's, and heavy black drapes over the windows, and Dixieland music and velvet throated crooners and shouters, and name-brand undiluted whiskey, and Southern fried chicken, and Chinese noodles, and barbecued spareribs with a secret sauce.

We sat opposite one another under pink indirect lights in an intimate booth and I watched her unabashedly tear at spareribs. Her mouth was red and wet, and shiny from the grease of the ribs. Her eyes were green and wide, her nose small and tilted, and her red hair was parted in the middle and cut short in a cap of tight glistening Grecian curls. Her dress matched her eyes, green with puffed sleeves, and a slit down the middle deeper than a pickpocket's reach. I watched her and hated the fact that she was grist for the mill, part of work, part of business, part of the chase after the ever-elusive buck.

She set down the rib, wiped her mouth with a napkin, sighed, said, "Somehow, Lover, I hate you."

"Me?"

"You. I've been waiting for you to open up. It's five nights now—and nothing."

"Open up?" I blinked over Scotch and water.

"Look. Let's face it. Nobody's name can be Timothy Tiddle. Not even yours. How'd I ever get to know you?"

"We were introduced, remember? By Phil Webster, the usual mutual acquaintance. You thought I was cute and I think you're lovely. What's the problem?"

"Timothy Tiddle, Texas oil millionaire. Brother, how corny can you get?"

I smiled around the rim of the glass. "What's corny?"

"You, pal. You're no visiting fireman. I'll say this for you. You spend like a Texas millionaire. You're a real welcome customer in my joint. Even the waiters like you, and my waiters are tough to please. But you're no fireman, pal. You're hip, real hip."

Demurely I said, "Little ole me?"

"Why, there ain't a joint in town, real joint, not the square joints, that you don't know and where you're not known. And just between you and me and a gnawed sparerib bone, you're not even on the make. I can tell. Your're just being polite, that's all, and gentlemanly, and squirelike. Now why in all hell *are* you squiring me around, kid? Break down and tell little Anabel."

The music was smooth now and there were couples tooling toward the dance floor. I put down my drink and pointed a finger over my shoulder. "Shall we?" I said. Gallantly.

She smiled with all the teeth. "The way you dance, I'd love it."

The floor was small, the lights dim, the music schmaltzy, and all of Anabel Jolly nestled beside me as we swayed on a dime, her mouth at my ear, and vice versa. She whispered, "What's your name, Lover?"

"Peter Chambers."

"You ready?"

There was a moment of silence. Then I said, "Yeah?"

"I knew it all the time."

"Knew what?"

"What your name was. Peter Chambers. I'm glad you finally told me."

I moved my head and looked at her. For the first time her eyes were pleased. She winked once, kissed me on the mouth lightly, and put her cheek against mine. Softly she said, "You're a figure around this town, pal. I played out the reel, waiting for action. You're a cop. A private dick, eye, richard—whatever the hell they call them. What's the promotion, pal? You looking to put a padlock on my joint?"

"No."

"I worked hard and I worked a long time to get where I am. I pay plenty ice. If I got to hist the ice, okay with me, you're on the payroll. Happens you're cute too. Happens I like you. You're liable to earn your fee, if you know what I mean." Her body pressed closer. "I'm not too hard to take, am I?"

"No."

"We got a deal?"

"No."

Her body went rigid. "Let's break it up, Lover."

We went back to our table. I said, "Anabel—"

"Don't Anabel me. You're looking to play it high and mighty, okay, then you're looking to have it catch up with you. I've handled tougher babies then you'll ever be."

"Maybe. But I've got nothing against your joint."

"Say that again, huh? Say it slow."

"Nothing against your joint. Period."

"Then what's the play?"

"Let me ask a few questions first. May I?"

"Shoot, Lover. I'm beginning to like you all over again."

"You're fixed pretty good for dough, aren't you?"

"The best."

"Like how?"

"Like I own the Club Jolly outright. Like I've got a hundred and fifty gees banked, in cash. Like I got a load of government bonds. Like I own a couple of apartment houses in L.A. Like I'm coining dough, every day, hand over fist. It wasn't this good always, but it's good now. I'm Number One in the strip racket. There's always a Number One. There is a Dempsey, a Ruth, a Tilden, a Valentino, a Garbo, a Pavlova—me, I'm Anabel Jolly. I'm doing a little bit of all right."

"Then what's with blackmail?"

The lids of the green eyes came down like purple shades. One corner of the mouth fought for a smile but it lost against the other corner: tight, and strained, and tense, and unhappy.

"Roger Aldridge," I said. "Six lousy letters. Two hundred and fifty thousand dollars."

"So that's it," she said.

"That's it."

"You working for him?"

"I'm trying."

The smile came, finally, bitter as though she'd bit into a worm. "A fine romance," she said.

"You and me?"

"That's the way I had it figured. You and me. That's the way I was born. I either go or I don't. With you I could go. I figured we could ring a couple bells together. Okay, so I figured wrong. G'bye, Lover."

"Roger Aldridge?"

"Go pick another doll to be a detective with. G'bye, Lover."

She stood up fast, tilting the table. I wrestled with it, righted it, and got out of the booth—but I was stopped by a waiter with the check. By the time I paid, she was gone. I came out of the warmth of pink dimness into the sad grey of sunless morning. A few early-go-to-workers straggled by. Traffic was sparse. City noise was muted. I whistled down a cab and I went home.

CHAPTER 2

Three o'clock in the office, I put through a call to Roger Aldridge. It was a fancy number, Plaza with a lot of circles. Everything about Roger Aldridge was fancy: his place of business, his mode of dress, his manner of living, his well-modulated voice—even the fee I was going to charge him, plus expenses. When the well-modulated voice came through, I said, "I've talked with her."

Tightly he said, "Save it."

"For when?"

"When can I see you?"

"Anytime. You're the client."

"Would you care to drop over to my apartment?"

"I'd care. When?"

"I can get away from the shop now. That is, if it's all right with you."

"You're still the client."

"You know the address of the apartment?"

"Yes."

"See you in about a half hour."

"Fine."

I hung up, rustled papers on the desk, clamped my lower lip between my fingers and tried to think about my fee, but my thoughts churned around Anabel Jolly. There was no doubt that Roger Aldridge could be touched up for a big figure. The guy was a buyer for a jewelry house, small and exclusive, but one of the top ten in the country. Yet, after all, he *was* an employee, and two hundred and fifty thousand blackmail bucks was a quarter of a million dollars, and that's not horsehair to fill a mattress. He was in good shape for the touch, what with a society wife of two years standing, a brand new kid, and a snobby job with a plush firm—but a quarter of a million is a quarter of a million—and like that you make it rough on yourself, Miss Anabel Jolly. You hit a guy for two bits, you might make it stick. But you hit a guy where it hurts, and he howls. Howling can't do you any good, Miss Anabel Jolly. Plus. Plus you don't need the dough. That makes it crazy. And when it's crazy you can't figure it—not without many more facts.

I didn't have much. I had a bare outline. Only what Aldridge had chosen to tell me. He had been recommended to me by an uncle (or I had been to him), an uncle named Donald Root, an old guy with a lot of loot, whose legs were withered and who lived in a wheel chair. Aldridge had told me about six steaming letters he had written to Jolly when he was hot on the make, about five years ago and before he was married. My job was to reconnoiter, mosey around, and find out what it was all about. If I could get back the letters without any trouble, it was worth fifteen thousand dollars. If not, it was my usual fee, plus expenses. I had not stated what my usual fee was and right now it was growing. My orders had been not to be in touch with him until I had something definite.

So I grabbed my hat and headed for Aldridge's place. I was either going to collect additional facts and really go to work on it, or I was going to collect my fast-growing fee and kiss it off. He lived on lower Fifth Avenue high up in a penthouse apartment, and a smooth-running elevator whisked me up rapidly. I applied an index finger to a mother-of-pearl doorbell, waited, and then the door was opened by a cute maid with a figure and dimples (this was a guy who kept begging for trouble). She said, "Yes?"

"Mr. Aldridge in?"

"Yes. Who may I say?"

"Peter Chambers."

"Please come in." She preceded me into a drawing room. She said, "Please make yourself at home. I will tell Mr. Aldridge you are here."

I said, "How long has he been here?"

"He just came in."

Aldridge's voice filtered through from a nearby room. "Who is it, Marie?"

The dimples deepened as she smiled at me. She said, "I'll tell him," and went out. Almost at once Aldridge was in the room and we were shaking hands.

"Prompt," he said. "I haven't even had a chance to wash. Don't blame me, do you, for not wanting to talk on the phone? Place of business, that sort of thing."

"Don't blame you in the least. Nice shack you've got here."

"Eleven rooms and it costs a fortune in rent, but if you don't put on the dog in my business, you're dead. Love you to meet my wife but she and the child are visiting her mother uptown. What do you drink, Mr. Chambers? If I don't have a splash, I'll blow up."

"Scotch and water. One cube."

He opened a cabinet and made drinks. He made mine first and handed it to me. For himself he poured half a tumbler of Scotch, added a spray of seltzer, and drank a lot of it in a hurry. He was tall and slim and about forty with blue-grey hair at the temples and a white mustache with waxed ends. He had blue eyes and a trick of squinting them at you when he talked. He said, "Any luck?"

I said "Hardly."

He didn't like that. He said, "Sit down." He was a man who was accustomed to giving commands. I didn't sit. I stood. He said, "What do you mean by 'hardly?' "

"Anabel Jolly. A hell of a gorgeous dame."

He smiled. Wryly. He said, "You're telling me?"

"Not the blackmail type at all."

"What does that mean?"

"Well, in my business, you can sort of spot them."

Brusquely he said, "Matter of opinion. Let's skip that, Mr. Chambers. Let's stick to the facts."

"Your the client."

"That's a pet phrase of yours, isn't it?"

"Anabel Jolly. She doesn't have to deal in blackmail. There we have a gal worth three-four hundred thousand bucks at a minimum figure. That's a matter of opinion too, but put that down as expert opinion, after investigation. I'd say a dame like that doesn't figure to resort to blackmail, aside from the fact that she's not the type."

"But the fact remains, Mr. Chambers, that she has."

"You've got me there, sir. It needs talking. And you've given me nothing to work on."

"Am I supposed to?"

"That's up to you. I'll say this, though. Unless you do, I'd rather you paid me my fee and we close up shop."

He finished his drink. "Fee? How much, Mr. Chambers?"

Now I squinted *my* eyes at *him.* "Fifteen days, fifty dollars a day, that's seven fifty, and I'll go easy on the expenses. Say, two fifty. That's a thousand dollars, round figure."

He put his glass down, opened his jacket and reached in for a narrow check book and a fountain pen. A holster hung from his belt and a gun was fixed in it.

I said, "You always wear that?"

"What?"

"The gun?"

"Yes. In my business, as I suppose in yours, it's a necessary evil. I frequently carry valuable jewelry on my person."

"You probably wear a gun more often than I do."

"Matter of fact, I always wear it. It's almost habit."

He wrote a check, ripped it out of the book and handed it to me. It was for a thousand dollars. He went back to the cabinet and made himself another drink. He said, "You're an independent cuss aren't you?"

I did a grin for him. "And an expensive one."

"That too. I don't mind the expense. I do mind a clash of temperaments."

"You don't have to be in love with a client to work for him. But you do need cooperation."

"Such as?"

"I might be able to help if you loosened up a little. You don't go to a doctor and then hold out on the symptoms."

He paced, glass in hand, sipped, and sat down. "You have a point there, sir."

"Thanks."

"Well, it's the old cornball deal of letters. Okay. Here's a dame got some hot letters of yours written five years ago. So what? Your wife, to whom you're married two years—she can't object to letters you wrote when you were single."

He twiddled with a point of his mustache. He said, "Those letters were undated, Mr. Chambers. Somehow, you don't date love letters—as though they were part of a business correspondence. When I had my interview with Miss Jolly at her club, she informed me that she would state that such letters were written within the past few months."

"Check," I said. "I'm sorry." I was beginning to warm up to Mr. Roger Aldridge. Maybe I was getting accustomed to his careful enunciation.

"Five years ago," he said and smiled, "I wasn't quite as conservative as I am now."

"What *was* the threat? Was she going to present them to your wife?"

"Better than that."

"Better . . . than . . . that?"

"A well-known press agent is contemplating a story on Miss Anabel Jolly for one of the tabloids. Miss Jolly threatens to turn my letters over to him—for added spice. Photostats, that sort of thing. Can you imagine the effect of such publication—on me?"

"Yeah," I said. I made myself another drink and sat down near him. "I can't figure it. Here's a dame that doesn't need the loot."

"Everybody needs a quarter of a million dollars."

"Not when it's attached to extortion. If you went to the cops with this and they worked out a plant—that's a felony, Mr. Aldridge. That dame can sit her sweet behind in the pokey for ten years on a deal like this. That's a crazy risk, I insist, when you don't need the loot."

"You sure about her monetary situation?"

"Positive. I put in ten days on that angle before I even met her. Why should a dame risk ten years out of the prime of her life when she absolutely doesn't need the money?"

He squinted at me and his teeth clicked along the edge of his glass. "You've got a point there."

"And why now? She's had that hot literature for five years. Why now, when she's sitting on top of the world, boss-lady of her own club?"

"You still working for me, Mr. Chambers?"

"If you say so."

"I say so."

"Then I'm still working for you."

Roger Aldridge abandoned his drink and stood up out of the chair. He went to a window, peered out, clasped his hands behind his back and spoke to me without looking at me. "I can't inform you about her need for money. I know nothing about that, pro or con. But I think I can answer your question."

"Which one?"

"The one about—why now."

"You mean there's a special reason why she's waited five years?"

"I don't know whether she's consciously waited for the right moment. But I do know that now—that this particular time in my career—is most propitious for this kind of holdup." He turned and came away from the window. "This is in the strictest confidence, Mr. Chambers."

"Of course."

"You know that I'm employed by Winston Parnell."

"Yes . . . ?"

"I earn a good deal of money now. About a hundred thousand dollars a year."

"Yes . . . ?"

I'm going to earn more than that."

"How?"

"Mr. Parnell is getting on in years. He's planning to retire. I am slated to take over the full active management of the firm. As a partner."

"I see."

"The lawyers have already prepared the papers. The date for the new partnership is November 15th. Miss Jolly got in touch with me early in October. She gave me until November 1st to make up my mind. I'm wondering if there's any connection."

"Yeah," I said brilliantly. "Yeah."

"You can imagine what will happen to me if this press agent scheme goes through. The notoriety would definitely finish the deal—since the papers, though prepared, are as yet unsigned. Do you understand now why it was worth fifteen thousand dollars to me to obtain the return of those blasted letters?"

"Yeah," I said. "But does Jolly know about . . . about this impending partnership?"

He shrugged expressive shoulders. "Frankly, I can't see how. The only ones who know about it are the principals and the lawyers. Except . . ." His Adam's apple jumped as he gulped.

"Who?"

"My cousin, Jonathan Nolan."

"That guy?" I said.

"He used to be a brilliant lawyer."

"Yeah, but he was disbarred last year, wasn't he?"

"Do you know him?"

"No, but I know about him. From your uncle."

"I have a great deal of confidence in Jonathan; that is, in his brain power. He's a young man, much younger than I, but, no matter what anyone may say about his morals, no one in the world can deny the fact of his brilliance."

"So?"

"When the contracts were finally prepared, I brought them to him for a last check."

"When was that?"

"Early in October."

"I get it. But . . . does he know Jolly?"

He nodded dejectedly. "He does. In fact, he introduced me to her."

"Think there's any connection?"

"This is the first time it's really occurred to me. Sounds stupid, but I simply cannot conceive of Jonathan having anything to do with blackmail. Jonathan would use a rapier rather than a bludgeon. No. Wide open blackmail would be too thickheaded for Jonathan, too blunt, and far too open to risk."

"Well, now that you *are* thinking about it . . ."

"At best guess—it could be—inadvertently perhaps—he dropped the information to Miss Jolly, and Miss Jolly decided to make hay in the sunshine."

"A quarter of a million. That's hay, all right."

"She's got me where it hurts. I'll tell you that, sir."

"Mind if I see Jonathan?"

He looked frightened. "If you think that's all right. But I don't think you ought to mention—"

"I agree with you. If he's in it, if he's using the bludgeon instead of the rapier—then he's in it. But if he's not, he might make an excellent advocate for the good Miss Jolly, once he learns about it. Though for the life of me I can't figure that gal. What's his address?"

"He has an apartment at 10 West 35th Street. And a small office at 150 West 42nd Street."

"And who's your lawyer?"

"Warren Dodge."

"The best. A fine old man. He's your uncle's lawyer, too, isn't he?"

"That's right."

"I'm going to talk with him, too. Does he know about your trouble with Jolly?"

"Nobody knows anything about that except you."

"I think we ought to take Mr. Dodge into our confidence."

He sat down and scraped a finger at a frown on his forehead. "You're the expert in these affairs, Mr. Chambers."

"Thanks," I said. "And thanks for the interview, and thanks for re-hiring me."

He took up his glass and drained it. He said, "I've got to do some tall thinking. Got the full day off tomorrow. Suppose I drop in at your office at about two o'clock."

"Sure."

I left him bent in his chair, staring at the floor and rubbing the same finger at the same frown on his forehead.

CHAPTER 3

The Flatiron Building is a skinny triangle pointing north on 23rd Street. Warren Dodge's office was on the 7th floor and an elderly lady at an ancient desk was his receptionist.

"Peter Chambers," I said, "for Mr. Dodge."

"Do you have an appointment, Mr. Chambers?"

"No, ma'am," I said.

She smiled and wrinkled her nose at me. "I don't know why I ask that question. It's silly. Please sit down. I'll ask Mr. Dodge if he'll see you." She pushed herself out of her chair, waddled to a door, opened it, and said, "There's a young man outside, Peter Chambers. Will you see him?"

Warren Dodge had a booming voice. "Sure I'll see him. I'd love to see him. Send him right in, Mamie, my girl. But you could have used the inter-com. That's what I've got it for."

"Inter-com." She sniffed. "Gadgets. People spending money for nothing. Giving themselves importance." She turned to me and smiled again. "Mr. Dodge would *love* to see you—even though you don't have an appointment. In here, please." She held the door open while I passed through, then slammed it behind me.

The office had wooden walls and many windows and green filing cabinets and a cluttered desk and the handsome Mr. Dodge behind the desk. Warren Dodge was at least seventy years of age but he looked fifty, acted forty, and had the zest of thirty. He was a bulky man with a smooth face, round and pink, and short cut tight grey hair. thick as steel wool and kinky as your aunt with arthritis. He was quick to laugh, his teeth were good, and the one eye that had begun to fail him was encased in a monocle.

"Good to see you, lad," he said. "And how goes it with all the little murderers in our fair city?"

"What a business," I said.

"You picked it."
"It's a living."
"You love it, Sir Knight of the Browbeaten." Buffed fingernails did a tatto on the desktop. "What's the occasion for a visit to a lawyer?"
"Roger Aldridge."
"Pompous but well-meaning. Known him since he's a boy."
"Old man Root recommended me."
"And I recommend you to Mr. Root a long time ago, while he was still active. What's Roger's trouble—that Mr. Root knows about?"
"Root doesn't know what Roger's trouble is. Roger told him he had need of a private detective and the old man mentioned me."
Warren Dodge stood up. "I smell gossip. I smell an enjoyable conversation. Let's get out of the would-be-businesslike atmosphere. Come into the library."
He opened a rear door and I followed him into a large cool book-lined room. There were easy chairs and a liquor cabinet and green blinds at the windows holding back the sun.
"Love this room," I said.
"Ancient. Most rooms, unlike most women, grow more beautiful with age." He chuckled. "Some day I'm going to fire Mamie and get me somebody with curves out there."
"You do all right."
"Well, I'm a bachelor, aren't I? And it happens I've retained my appreciation for curves."
"Know Anabel Jolly?"
"No. Should I?"
"But curves."
"Then I should."
"Roger Aldridge knows her."
"That the trouble?"
"That's it."
"You free to tell me about it?"
"Yes."
He chuckled again. "Told you I smelled gossip. Sit down. Let me fix a couple of long ones. You're a Scotchman, aren't you?"
"Yes, sir." I moved into a soft leather chair and stretched my legs.
Warren Dodge said, "One cube, if I remember."
"There's not much you forget, sir."
He brought the drinks, set them up on a corner of a library table, backed into a nearby easy chair, opened the laces of his shoes, kicked them off, sighed, took up his

drink, said smilingly, "Make it gory, lad . . . or make it sexy."

I told him the story from the time I'd been retained by Roger Aldridge, and his first comment was: "Sounds fascinating, that Anabel Jolly."

"Is fascinating."

"You reserving that?"

"I am."

"For whom?"

"For me."

His eyes grinned. "Too bad. All right, what's this visit for?"

"Well . . . since we both know some of the parties involved . . . I thought it might be good sense to talk it over with you. I come for advice, Mr. Dodge, and for counsel."

"What are you really here for, Peter?"

"I'd like the lowdown on Jonathan Nolan."

"That's better." He took the monocle out, breathed on it, wiped it with a handkerchief, set it back. "Jonathan Nolan. I'm inclined to agree with Roger. I don't think he'd tamper with blackmail. He's too shrewd, too careful, and . . . too imaginative."

"What's the story on that guy, Mr. Dodge?"

"Brilliant. Too brilliant. Too wise. Too worldly. Too acquisitive. Wanting to get rich, really rich, too quickly."

"How old a guy?"

"Jonathan? Now? Not more than thirty, all told. Brilliant student, quick early success—then, bang."

"How'd the bang happen?"

"Let's begin at the beginning, eh?"

"It's your story, sir."

"Jonathan Nolan." He sighed and the eye behind the monocle closed in reminiscence. "A wild kid and headstrong. An orphan, as was Roger. Brought up by the uncle, Donald Root—both of them. These two boys are his only legal heirs, his only heirs-at-law. Two boys reared in the same environment, one crazy-wild, the other quiet and stuffy."

"About Jonathan . . . ?" I said.

"He got out of law school, very early, at the age of twenty-two. That was about the time Donald Root's wife died. At that time, Mr. Root gave up his estate in Scarsdale, and took his apartment in town. You know where he lives, an old-fashioned narrow little house on Park Avenue. A splendid old house, five stories high, but nothing pretentious, no doorman, self-service elevator—quiet and dignified. And there Mr. Root lives to this day, an invalid now, attended only by Emerson Beach, valet, cook, and chauffeur."

"About Jonathan . . . ?" I said.

"He gave each of them a present, the younger Jonathan and the older Roger . . . fifty thousand dollars each . . . and they were on their own, living apart, no longer part of the household."

"Now, about Jonathan . . . ?"

"As you know—I am aware that Mr. Root took you into his confidence—his will only mentioned them . . . Jonathan and Roger . . . to share alike of his estate upon his decease." He held up a hand as though warding off a brickbat. He said, "Yes, yes . . . about Jonathan. He practiced law, and he practiced it in a hurry . . . but he was a professional boxer, for a while, on the side."

I felt my eyebrows fly up. "A professional boxer?"

"He had been intercollegiate heavyweight champ. Friends prevailed on him to enter the professional domain. He did, felt he wasn't good enough and went back to practicing law in a hurry."

"What do you mean . . . practicing law in a hurry?"

"Obtaining negligence cases through unethical means, handling unsavory cases that other lawyers wouldn't handle . . . making a lot of money, and always spending a bit more than he earned . . . and gathering a bad reputation along the way. Donald Root called him in and warned him. As did the bar association after several complaints. Then he became a boxing manager."

"A *boxing* manager."

"Behind-the-scenes boxing manager, but it heralded an era of more fixed fights than the boxing business had ever known. Again he made a good deal of money, and again he spent a good deal of money . . . but it finally caught up with him. His sheer brilliance, his planning, his cunning . . . prevented his going to jail. Six others were found guilty, and sentenced . . . but there was insufficient evidence for his conviction, and he was acquitted."

"Any money left?"

"Very little. But the bar association didn't need the quality of evidence required by a criminal court—proof of guilt beyond a reasonable doubt. And certain evidence that, in our jurisprudence, was inadmissible in a court of law, *was* admissible to the bar association sitting in committee. Jonathan Nolan was disbarred."

"When?"

"One year ago. And at that time—as I remember Mr. Root informed you—he changed his will. Jonathan was cut off. One half of Mr. Root's estate goes to Roger Aldridge, the remainder to charity. A simple half page will replaced the old one."

"And how's Jonathan fixed for money at the present?"

"Not too well from what I hear."

"What's he doing now?"

"He's a bookmaker."

"A *what*?"

"A bookmaker."

I finished my drink and I stood up. "Good-bye, Mr. Dodge."

"Where to now, lad?"

"Jonathan Nolan."

"Careful does it."

"Careful? Why?"

"He hits first and asks questions later—he's the type. And he's thoroughly capable."

"Thanks for the information." I winked at him and waved my hand. "And thanks for the advice. Take care."

"You too."

CHAPTER 4

The black wall bulletin in the lobby of 150 West 42nd Street said J. NOLAN . . . 1401 . . . in white celluloid replaceable letters. The elevators were in the rear and I went there and waited amongst a small knot of prospective passengers. The elevator arrived with a rattle like dungeon chains and we entered and each of us sounded off with his floor number. I got out at 14 and walked a long narrow corridor to 1401. It was a door with a glaze-glass window and no printing on it except the number: 1401. Adjacent was another door of metal, stating in red letters: STAIRWAY. I tried that door first. It opened on a stairway landing, cool, dim and deserted. I closed the door and tried 1401. It gave on one push.

I was in a square room with a stone floor and no furniture except a narrow desk with a swivel chair behind it and a wooden armchair in front of it. There was a covey of five telephones on the desk, an ashtry, and a long pad of yellow foolscap with a pencil on it. That was it.

A tall young man was pacing the floor when I entered. He was broad-shouldered and lithe with black hair parted on the side, black eyes, a firm jaw, a jutting chin, and a pale face. He wore an Oxford grey suit, a white button-down shirt, and a yellow and black striped tie. The suit had a vest. There was a chain going from pocket to pocket of the vest and a gold boxing glove hung from the middle of the chain.

He threw me a quick look, lifted a smooth black eyebrow, went to the swivel chair, slid down, injected a thin cigar into a corner of his mouth and cocked it like a field gun.

I said, "Jonathan Nolan?"

"That's right." He angled the chair, lifted his legs, banged his heels on the desktop and left them there.

My cue was to work out a connection, if any, between Jonathan Nolan and Anabel Jolly, and my tactic was quick-job chatter and see what happens. I said: "Anabel sent me."

Color came up in his face and stayed there like a stuck elevator. His heels scraped off the desk. The chair straightened and he leaned forward. "Come again?"

"Anabel Jolly."

"Who the hell is Anabel Jolly?"

"A twist—with a twist. Who happens to be cutting me in. Which is why I come to see you. You and me, we're supposed to talk."

The elevator came unstuck. Color receded from his face.

"Talk? Talk about what?"

"Quiet money."

"What kind of money?"

"There's people call it blackmail. There's all kinds of operators—amateurs. I'm a professional. Quiet money is my business. Ask Anabel. You move up to the kind of money that counts, you need the professional touch. Me, that's what I got, the professional touch. Anabel says I'm to see you. So I'm seeing you."

"What's your name?"

"Bellows. Gus Bellows."

The black eyes stayed on mine, then dropped. The right hand went to the jacket pocket and for a moment I thought I was going to have gun trouble. But the hand came up with a packet of matches, and I relaxed. He lit the point of the cigar and flung the packet onto the desk. He puffed, hard, until there was a good deal of smoke between us and the point of the cigar flattened to a red blaze. Then he flung it, burning end forward, right at my face, and as I jumped to duck, he came after it, one spring over the desk. A thick right jolted me to the floor. Two hands grabbed the hair of my head, raised it and smashed the back of it against the stone floor. His face bulged out in front of me, and whirled . . . then blackness.

CHAPTER 5

One leg moved first, then the other leg, then I heard a groan. I lay flat on my back and listened. I heard another groan and then another before I realized it was I who was groaning, so I stopped. My legs moved again and I tried to get up but I couldn't make it. I rolled over, prone. There was a numbness in back of my head. I pulled my knees up under me and pushed the cold floor with my knees and my hands and my forehead and I began to come up, the middle of me first, lumped up like a camel; but then I got tired and I dropped. I rested on my face, a throbbing replacing the numbness in the back of my head. Then I did it again, the same way, knees and hands and forehead pushing, back end coming up first. Then I got my forehead off the floor, got a foot under me, grabbed at a ledge with my hand, and pulled myself up. I heard the slap of something dropping but I didn't care. I was facing a wall, and I leaned on it, panting. Then I began to breathe more deeply. I was able to shake my head against oncoming nausea. I fought it down, shaking my head all the time like a dog out of water. The area stopped swaying and levelled off.

I was on the landing on the other side of the door marked STAIRWAY. The ledge that my hand was holding was the bannister. I let go, touched the back of my head, and looked at my hand. It was dry. I looked down to see what had dropped. There were two things. There was my wallet and my credentials as an investigator. The good Mr. Nolan must have thrown those into my lap, like you throw a sneer at a wise guy when the wise guy turns out to be stupid, and I had turned out to be just that. I had had action from Mr. Nolan before I had expected action. Faintly, I promised myself that the action between Mr. Nolan and myself had only begun.

Double vision hit me again. I didn't stoop for my stuff and wallet. Instead, I slid down to the top step, sat, stuck my head deep down between my knees, and drew big sops of breath. I sat like that for ten minutes and I began to feel better. I reached for the wallet, shoved the stuff into it, put the wallet into a pocket and pulled myself up to standing. I opened the door and I was out in the corridor. I fell against 1401, turned the knob and pushed, but it was locked. I stumbled to the elevator, fluttering like a loose pair of drawers hung out in a stiff breeze. I leaned against the button and then the elevator came and the door slung open, and the operator's face got long with worry.

"What happened?" he said. "What happened, bub?"

"Slipped in the hall. Banged my head."

"Get in, bub. We'll go down express. Talk to the starter."

Downstairs, the starter said, "Was there anything wrong up there, anything slippery? I'll send the boy up for a look. Anything wrong, you put in a claim. We run this building de luxe. I'll make a report on it right way."

"No. Nothing wrong. No report. Just got my two left feet mixed up. My own fault. If you'd help me to a cab, I'd appreciate it."

"Sure, Jack."

I gave the cabbie my doctor's address and fifteen minutes later I was sprawled under an X-ray machine. I was feeling much better. He had given me a shot in the arm, a pill to swallow, and water to drink that had tasted as lousy as all water tastes from a paper container. Then he had touched my head, murmured about "Hematoma," and led me to the X-ray machine. I rested on a cot while the plates were being developed. Then the doctor came to me, smilingly.

"Nothing harder than a hard head," he informed me. "You had me concerned for a while but there's no fracture. Nevertheless I want you off your feet for a couple of hours. Will you do that for me?"

"Not here. I'm allergic to cots since the Army."

"No. I'll take you upstairs, put you up in a nice comfy bedroom, give you a nice comfy pill, and you'll sleep for a nice comfy couple of hours."

I looked at my watch. It was a nice comfy six o'clock.

"Okay," I said

Upstairs, with my clothes off, in bed with a pillow under my head, I staved off the pill with upraised hand. "Can I make a couple of phone calls first?"

"Sure."

"Phone book?"

"Sure."

He brought me a phone book and took his pill away with him. I looked up Jonathan Nolan on West 35th Street. I dialed the number. There was no answer. Then I called Warren Dodge at home. He answered quickly. I said, "Mr. Dodge, one question."

"Who is this?"

"Peter Chambers."

"What's your question, son?"

"Jonathan Nolan. He married?"

"Bachelor."

"He still live at 10 West 35th Street?"

"That's right."

"Thanks, Mr. Dodge."

"That all?"

"That's all."

"Real mysterious."

"Got to go to sleep now. Thanks, Mr. Dodge."

"Sleep? I beg your pardon? What? What was that?"

"Bye, now. Thanks."

I hung up. I called Nolan's number again. I let it ring a long time. There was no answer. Then I checked the phone book for M. Russell, Locks and Keys, 850 Sixth Avenue. I called the number and it was answered on one ring. I said, "Mel?"

"Just a minute."

Another voice came on. "Hello?"

"Mel?"

"Yeah."

"Pete."

"Pete who?"

"Pete Chambers."

The voice brightened. "Hi, shamus."

"You free right now?"

"Always free for you, shamus. You're my boy."

"I need a job, quick and clean. But you've got to go out on it right away. Name's Jonathan Nolan. Address 10 West 35th Street. I want a key to get in. You're gonna have to slip up there fast for an impression job. He's not home now, so now is fine. I just called him. You call, just for a double check, before you start working your magic. He's in the phone book. Got it, pal?"

"Got it, pal."

"Go to it."

"When do you want delivery?"

"Tonight. Will your wife let you out tonight?"

I could feel his grin. "Not if she knows it's with you. I'll tell her it's poker."

"Fine. I'll meet you at eleven o'clock. Club Jolly. Okay?"

"You twisted my arm."

"Okay. Go to work." I hung up. I called: "Doc." He came into the room. I said, "All right, put me to sleep. But I've got to be up at ten-thirty."

"Depend on me. Now stick your tongue out."

He put a pill on it and I gulped water.

CHAPTER 6

Club Jolly was jumping. The band was beating it up like the bennies were being overworked. Cigarette smoke put a ceiling under the ceiling. The customers were buzzing, the waiters were scampering for drinks, the tiny dance floor was getting a workout (as were the dancers), and an aura of expectation quivered over the joint; it was eleven o'clock. Anabel Jolly went on at eleven-thirty; then it was each hour on the half-hour, four times after that.

I waited at a wall table. Then the maître d' brought Mel Russell down to me, Mel in a blue serge suit and a wide grin. He sat down beside me and ordered a drink. I said, "How'd it go?"

"Wrap-up. It's apartment 2E. Happy hunting." He produced a key and handed it to me.

"That all?" I said.

"One key. Period."

"How much?"

"Twenty-five bucks. For you. And I split the tab here."

"Never mind that. The tab here's on me. Enjoy." I paid him, and put the key in my pocket.

"Anabel Jolly," he said. "Wow."

"Have you seen her?"

"Nope—but I've heard."

The music ceased. The dancers straggled back to their tables. The curtains closed, the dim lights grew dimmer, there was a roll on the drums, and a blue spot played on the shimmering curtains. Then the curtains parted again, the music grew torchy and Anabel Jolly's warm-up appeared: a slender girl with a bosom as flat as old beer and a throaty voice. She sang six sick love songs, and went away. Once more the curtains closed, this time the dimness turned to black, and then the curtains parted to a blue spotlight on Anabel Jolly.

When it was over, Mel Russell wiped sweat from his brow and said, "Murder."

"Would you like to meet her?"

"Brother, would I?"

I sent the waiter back with a message, and the waiter came back with a message for me. "Miss Jolly," he said, "says no."

Mel said, "You're slipping."

"Must be," I said. "You want to sit around and see it over?"

"How long?"

"An hour."

"Do you?"

"I'm going. I've got a headache. In back of my head."

"You're really slipping, Pete. Time was you couldn't be pried out of a joint like this till closing."

"Yeah," I said. "You want to substitute for me?"

"Substitute? What kind of substitute?"

"Female substitute."

"Sure." A grin wrinkled his face. "As long as I'm playing poker . . ."

I paid the check, tipped the waiter, shook hands with Mel, and on the way out I tipped the maître d' and whispered to him, pointing toward Mel.

"Leave it to me," said the maître d'.

Outside, I used a phone booth in an all-night drug store. I called Jonathan Nolan. There was no answer. I rubbed at a sharp pain in the back of my head, had an argument with myself and lost. I decided to go home and go to bed.

CHAPTER 7

At two o'clock in the afternoon, Roger Aldridge presented himself at my office. There was a criss-cross of bags beneath his eyes and his doleful expression had an aspect of failure like a husband about to commence an argument with his wife. "I believe," he said, "my initial error was bringing those contracts to Jonathan. The more I think about it, the more I believe that move precipitated this series of events. But it's easy to be wise—after the fact."

"Second guessers never win."

"Be that as it may, I am very near a decision."

"You're the client."

"I'm going to pay, Mr. Chambers."

"Pardon?"

"I'm going to pay up and shut up. What do you say to that?"

"I say you're nuts."

"Why?"

"Because blackmail never ends."

"But I'd get back those letters. That's all she has—that's irrefutable."

"She can make photostats. It can go on and on."

"No," he said. "I'd pay, and effect the return of six letters." Then, coldly, he added: "If she monkeyed with me after that—I'd kill her."

"Simple as that?"

"Yes. Essentially I'm a meek man. I'm willing to compromise—"

"Two hundred and fifty thousand dollars. That's a hell of a lot of compromise."

"But even the meekest of us, jockeyed into a corner, and then pushed . . . we'll jump. I'll make a business deal with her but if after that, she tries any funny stuff—I'll kill her. I'm going to make that perfectly clear to her."

I lit a cigarette. I said, "How's it figure, Mr. Aldridge?"

"A partnership in Winston Parnell would mean approximately three hundred thousand dollars a year to me. The kind of notoriety she plans would of course, wreck it. I consider it good business therefore, in these circumstances, to pay the equivalent of one year's earnings to protect such earnings for the remainder of my working life. Do you see my point, sir?"

"Yes, I suppose I do. Have you got that kind of dough? To spare?"

"Frankly, I don't. I earn a good deal of money, but what with taxes and my necessary mode of living—my savings are meager."

"Then how do you propose to pay it?"

"I've decided to discuss it with my uncle. You know about his will."

"Yes."

"It's common knowledge . . . well, family knowledge . . . that's he's worth at least a million dollars, in cash. It is also no secret that half of that goes to me upon his death, the other half to charity. I'm going to ask him to advance two hundred and fifty thousand dollars from my half right now . . . as a loan . . . to be returned by me in three yearly installments."

"You going to tell him what it's about?"

"I'm going to tell him the entire story. Which brings me to another point. I should like a favor of you."

"Me? At the prices you're paying—a pleasure."

"My uncle has a great deal of confidence in you. I have an appointment with him for three o'clock. I should like you to come there, say . . . at five . . . five o'clock. You'll corroborate my facts. And today's the best day to talk with him."

"Why today?"

"It's Emerson Beach's day off."

"Beach?"

"His valet."

"Oh yes."

"Beach leaves in the morning and doesn't return until five o'clock. That gives me two hours alone with my uncle, just the two of us, all alone. Then you'll come and I've also asked Warren Dodge to drop by. Like that, my uncle will know the whole story, and he'll be able to have a rounded view, the opinion of each of us. Will you come, Mr. Chambers?"

"Sure."

"Thank you. Thank you very much."

He rose and we shook hands and he went away. I killed my cigarette and went to the window. I saw him come out of the building and hail a cab. Another cab, parked at the curb, shot out after his. I had a hunch that Roger Aldridge had grown a tail.

CHAPTER 8

Donald Root lived on Park Avenue near 69th Street. It was a white edifice, a midget between giants, a narrow building of five stories between two skyscrapers, a symbol of the individuality of the stubborn owner who refused to dispose of his property (at fabulous offers) at the constant behest of the builders for the cliffdwellers. Donald Root owned the property but he occupied but one apartment.

The structure had none of the Park Avenue trappings. There was no doorman, no inside man, no starched dickeys, no canopy, no downstairs switchboard. You opened a brassbound, glass-brick door to a small, immaculate lobby. There was a marble floor, a mahogany side table, a lamp, a mirror, a self-service elevator, and a cool silence. Each floor had one apartment of five rooms, and each tenant was a carefully selected individual of means and culture.

It was exactly five o'clock when the elevator slid open for me. I pushed the button for 4, rose silently and emerged to a carpeted foyer. There was one door, the door to Donald Root's apartment, and the door was ajar. I pushed a button which produced a two-tone tinkle, but produced nothing else. I repeated the two-tone tinkle, waited, then shoved in. I went through a small vestibule into a vast drawing room. Donald Root was in his wheel chair behind his desk. There was a small hole in his forehead and his lifeless chin drooped on his chest.

Roger Aldridge was sprawled face down on the thick red carpet. There was a gun in his hand.

I moved fast. The gun was Roger's gun; his holster was empty. He had a blue welt on his forehead over his right eye. His position was such that he seemed to have been going away; his head was toward the door. The point of one shoe was wedged in a slit of the red carpet where the carpet appeared to be torn. I looked up. There was a bullet hole in the ceiling.

The bullet hole in the ceiling convinced me. I stooped, tore out a tuft of the red carpet, pocketed it and went to Donald Root. I put my ear against his heart to listen for a beat because that is the thing to do, but there was no question. Donald Root was dead. And the expression on his face had died with him: surprise and fear. I lifted the chin and looked at more of the face: surprise and fear. I let the chin go and touched a finger to the paper in front of him on the desk. It was his will and he had just changed it. His fountain pen was still in his rigid hand.

I read the will quickly. It was entirely in the handwriting of Donald Root. It was the will he had told me about, the one Warren Dodge had mentioned, a half page deal, leaving half his estate to Roger Aldridge and the other half to charity. There was no residual clause. It was signed, and attested by two witnesses. But he had added to it. Beneath his signature, between the attestation clause and the signatures of the witnesses, he had added, in his own handwriting:

> "I hereby bequeath an additional two hundred and fifty thousand dollars to my nephew, Roger Aldridge."

That was all. There was nothing else.

I bent over, examining the carpet at the point in which Roger's shoe was caught, and that was my position when I thought I heard the elevator door open and close. I was slapping at Roger's face, slapping him back to consciousness, when I saw two feet standing near me. I looked up to the white-pale face of Emerson Beach.

"What . . . ?" he gasped. "What's happened?"

"This is the way I found them. Five minutes ago."

His fingers trembled in the direction of Donald Root. "Is he . . . ? Is he . . . ?"

"He's dead. You'd better call the police. Right now."

CHAPTER 9

One hour later Roger Aldridge had been booked for murder and I was frantically trying to find Warren Dodge. I showed up at the Flatiron Building just as Mamie was closing up shop.

"You've been calling and calling," she said.

"Have you heard from him?"

"No, I haven't. But that's not unusual. He left rather late."

"When?"

"He left here at four-thirty."

"Did he say where he was going?"

"To Donald Root's."

"He never showed up there."

"That's not unusual, either. Mr. Dodge frequently gets detoured."

Just then the phone rang. Mamie picked it up, said hello, listened. Her mouth opened and she turned greener than a yokel with his last drink on his first binge. She hung up. She said, "He's in a hospital."

"Where?"

"The Flower."

We didn't say a word to each other as the cab fought the going-home traffic. At the hospital I paid and we ran up the steps. We inquired at the office, and the elevator took us to the eleventh floor. A young doctor said, "You first," to Mamie.

I said, "May I see him, too?"

"Wait here. We'll be out in a few moments."

I paced the corridor trying to forget the hospital smells and then they were out of his room and coming toward me, and Mamie was wiping her eyes with a handkerchief.

"I told him you were here," she said. "He wants to see you. He's ordered me to go home."

"Nothing you can do here," the young doctor said. "He's to stay at least overnight, perhaps more."

Mamie squeezed my arm, then turned away and proceeded toward the elevators. To the young doctor I said, "What happened?"

"Emergency when we picked him up. Severe concussion and a bad gash, eleven stitches in his head. He shouldn't see visitors but he insists on you. Don't stay more than five minutes."

The smell of ether was strong in the room. The bed was cranked up to a half-sitting position. Warren Dodge had his eyes closed and his face was paper-white. He looked naked without his monocle. Bandages and adhesive tape made a tight skull cap on his head. He opened his eyes, saw me, tried for a smile and missed. He said, "Hi, Peter."

"Hi."

His eyes slid to the doctor. "I want to talk to my friend. Alone, if you please."

"No more than five minutes."

I nodded and the doctor went out.

"What happened?" I said.

Weakly he said, "I was slugged."

"Where?"

"The downstairs lobby at Donald Root's."

"Who slugged you?"

"I told the police I didn't know. I was slugged from behind."

"Robbery?"

"No."

His eyes closed again and there was silence except for the rattle in his throat from his breathing. Then his eyes opened.

I said, "Slugged. But why? What motive?"

He winked, but if he was trying for jauntiness, it misfired. He looked tired and old and pathetic. He said, "I told the police I didn't know who but I do."

"Then why didn't you tell them?"

"Because it would have been my word against his and that's no good. It's not proof. And he doesn't think I know which is good. It gives us a weapon." He shook his head slowly. "I don't understand it."

"What happened, Mr. Dodge? We've only got five minutes."

"I want you to work on it, lad. Bill me if necessary."

"I'll work on it. But let's have the story."

He drew a deep breath, and exhaled in an ether-smelling blast. "I was due at Mr. Root's. I was a little early. I entered the lobby and pushed the button for the elevator. The indicator showed it was at 4. I turned my back on it as it was coming down. I was wiping my monocle when the blow came. The elevator had opened and a passenger had stepped out. As the blow came I glanced upward at the mirror and I saw him. Then it struck. It was the back end of a pistol. For the life of me I can't understand it. That's your job, Peter. If I ever get out of here, I want to know why he struck me. He doesn't know I saw him."

"Who, for heaven's sake?"

"Jonathan Nolan."

CHAPTER 10

Detective-lieutenant Parker tilted his chair back and blew cigar smoke. Parker, out of Homicide, was a straight cop with no angles. He set the chair back on its four legs, leaned his elbows on the desk, and said, "Who's the dame, Pete?"

"Dame?" I said.

"Dame, gal, girl, quiff. Who was holding Aldridge up for blackmail?"

"Oh, that dame."

"Yeah, that dame."

"Aldridge wouldn't tell you, would he?"

"No."

"Then how do you expect me to? I play ball but I don't stool on a client. You know that."

"Yes, I know it." He sat back and smoked his cigar. His office was small and neat. He looked it over and then his eyes came back to me. "Very gallant, Roger Aldridge. Part of his story is good, part of it stinks."

"Matter of opinion. What's his story? To you?"

"Same as it's been to you, pal."

"Well, let's hear your version."

"Dame was holding him up for a quarter of a million and he'd decided to pay it. Went to the uncle for a big loan. Was talking with the uncle, all alone, when the bell tinkled. Went to answer the door but there seemed to be nobody there. Suddenly, he got hit a blow on the forehead. The lights went out for him. When he came to, the old man was dead, the will was changed and the gun was in his hand. His own gun. That's *his* story."

"What's your story, Lieutenant?"

"Mine has a lot of evidence to back it up, which is why dear Roger is in the can."

"Where do the two stories differ?"

"Not at the beginning. We accept the first part of his story—that he went to the old man for dough. But from there on in, we see it different. We say the old man refused the loan. We say Aldridge got ideas. We say he used his gun as a threat for the old man to change his will. Under duress, the old man did just that. Then we say Aldridge knocked him off. Ballistics prove the bullet was from that gun. Serial number shows it was his gun. Paraffin shows he fired it. Then, we say, he tried to beat it, got his foot tangled in the carpet in his hurry to get out. It tore, and he flopped, hit his head, passed out, and that's how you found him."

"What about the bullet in the ceiling?"

"Missed, the first try."

"Pretty wide miss."

"Could happen when you're excited."

"Did you examine that torn carpet?"

"We examine everything."

"Could it have been cut rather than torn?"

"Could have been, but we say it was torn. He'd have to prove different."

"Would a guy use his own gun to commit murder?"

"He had it on him, he admits it. We say the idea was an impulse. We say he was on his way to get rid of it."

"Would he have invited me to come there?"

"Same answer. The idea shaped up as impulse. He'd have been out of there, if he hadn't tripped himself, before either you or the butler would have shown up. Why do you look at me cockeyed like that? You got a better story?"

"Not yet I don't."

"Hope to have?"

"Maybe. If and when—I'll let you know. By the way, you keeping Aldridge here overnight?"

"Yep."

"Will I be able to see him?"

"Why not?"

"I'll say this, Lieutenant. You're a gentleman."

"It's just as easy . . ."

"Okay, pal, thanks. And don't go overboard."

"Why?"

"Because maybe I *have* a story coming up."

"Make it a good one, shamus. You generally do."

"I'll try, Lieutenant. I'll do my best."

"It's gonna be tough."

"It's been tougher. Thanks for letting me talk to you."

CHAPTER 11

Anabel Jolly lived in a penthouse on Central Park South. I had taken her home several times but only to the door;

I had never been in the apartment. It was on the 16th floor, with an orange lacquered door, and a sliding peephole with a mirrored front. She figured to be in. Anabel Jolly went to sleep in the morning; for her, then, evening was early afternoon. But she had run out on me at Jackson's and she had refused to see me at the Jolly—so I wasn't taking any chances.

The elevator took me up to the 16th floor, just the two of us, the young driver and myself. I said, "Do you know if Miss Jolly is in?"

"I think so. I ain't taken her out."

"Will you ring her bell, please?"

"Bell? What for?"

"Deliver a message."

He put a stay against the elevator door and left it open. In the aisle near her door he said: "What's the message, mister?"

"Me."

"What?"

"I'm the message."

His eyebrows moved down. "I don't get it."

I took a twenty dollar bill out of my wallet, waved it once and slowly, folded it and handed it to him. "You ring the bell, she flips the peephole, she sees it's you, you say you got a message and I take it over from there. Okay?"

Now his eyebrows were up and his grin was a half grin, tentative but costly. I added a twenty to the twenty and he was convinced. He improved on my directions. He rang the bell and we waited. Then the peephole moved, an eye was applied, and Anabel's voice said, "What is it, Oscar?"

"Got a package for you, ma'am."

The door opened and I wedged a foot in. Then I shoved hard on the door, knocked her back, entered and shut the door behind me. And locked it. She came toward me, her green eyes hot with fury.

"Easy does it," I said. "Remember me? We were going to ring bells together. Timothy Tiddle."

"Bells," she said. "Balls."

"Easy, baby."

"What the hell do you think you're trying to pull here?"

Think? Who could think? Anabel Jolly was wearing a negligée and high-heeled house shoes. The house shoes were pink and open at the toes. The negligée was diaphanous. Diaphanous. If diaphanous is gauzy pink transparence, if diaphanous is a beautifully carved white marble moving statue veiled in the sheerest pink, if diaphanous improves the unimprovable, enhances the unenhanceable, sets the heart to hammering and beats the blood to the brain—then diaphanous is the word.

She kept coming at me, the wild green fury in her eyes and her hands out like claws. I grabbed her. Mostly in self-defense. Mostly. But not all. I grabbed her by the wrists, and forced her hands behind her and into the small of her back, bending her forward and toward me until her body was tight against mine, and then I captured her mouth with my mouth, and she struggled hard as I kissed her, and then she didn't struggle quite so hard, and then she didn't struggle at all.

I released her soft wet lips and moved my mouth to her ear. I said, "I'm not breaking in here to play potsy. A guy's been murdered, and your name's liable to crop up at any moment. That's why I'm here."

Then I let her go.

She remained where she was, motionless, her hands at her sides, the shine of faint tears in her eyes, the soft curves of her body molded to mine. Then her hands moved up and touched my cheeks and lightly, sweetly, without suction, she kissed a corner of my mouth. Then she smiled and said, "Come in, punk."

A breeze from the terrace rustled through the living room. There were rose lights, and three large divans with many silk pillows, and two contiguous walls were entirely of amber-colored blocks of mirror. There was a fireplace and andirons and easy chairs and a bar and gay stools and an original *Cobelle* on one wall. Anabel moved about, pacing, flouncing, nervously slapping open palms against resonant hips, then she dropped into an easy chair and crossed her long legs and now the white marble of one thigh was exposed, gleaming in the rose light of the room. She said, "What's it all about, Lover?"

"Roger Aldridge."

Her expression tightened. "You still butting into that?"

"It's beyond that now."

"Beyond what?"

"My butting in."

"I don't understand."

"Do you know Donald Root?"

"No."

"Ever hear of him?"

"No."

I brought her a cigarette, breathed her perfume as I lit it for her, and lit one for myself.

She said, "Sit here. Near me."

I sat where the view was better. Across from her.

I told her about Donald Root. I told her about Roger Aldridge. I told her about Jonathan Nolan. I told her about Warren Dodge. I filled her in from the time I was retained to right now. If she was hustling for blackmail, then my hunch was wrong, and I'd tipped my mitt—and let her take advantage of me. I said exactly that, and I was through. I sat back and let her take it from there.

She didn't move. Her legs were uncrossed now, her knees apart, the pink negligée ruffled in little mounds at her heels. Her pinky was in her mouth and she was biting at the fingernail and the tiny pucker between her eyes was a frown.

She said, "Thanks for the vote of confidence."

"Skip it."

She said, "You're nice."

"Skip that too."

She said, "You think Roger killed his uncle?"

"No."

She said, "You're sweet."

"Honey, we haven't got time for that kind of stuff now."

She stood up, suddenly, wrapped the negligée around her, turned, and slowly walked away, swayingly. My breath caught in my throat. It was something to see diaphanous pink around a fascinating rise of firm white undulant marble. Then she was out of the room and I jumped for the bar and snatched another drink for resuscitation. I was in the process of snatching another drink for further resuscitation when she returned. She placed a folded packet in my hand and she said, "You just earned yourself fifteen thousand dollars. Thanks again for the vote of confidence."

I don't unfold the packet.

She said, "Six letters. From Roger Aldridge to Anabel Jolly. Original letters. There ain't no copies, no photostats, no nothing."

I slipped the packet into a pocket. I said, "What's the story, Miss Jolly?"

"Miss Jolly, huh?" She glared at me, crinkle-eyed. "Real stranger, all of a sudden. What's the matter? Fifteen thousand bucks go to your head?" Then she moved to a divan, turned, said, "Sorry," turned back, threw herself on it, lay there prone, every curve of her accentuated, and cupped her chin in her hands. I still had that second drink in my hand. I gulped it fast and got rid of the glass. She said: "I don't know *what* the story is. But I can tell you my end."

"Let's have it, huh?"

Her hands moved out from under her chin. She cocked

a finger, beckoned with it, then patted the divan beside her. "Come here, Lover."

I went. Because it was business.

I sat rigid beside her and listened.

She turned on her side as she talked. "Roger wrote these things a long time ago. I save that kind of stuff. For laughs. That's all the guy ever was to me—a couple of laughs. I pick my men. And they're few and far between. It's got to be a guy that gives me a tingle, a jingle, a guy I can ring bells with."

"So?"

"Who can ring bells with Roger Aldridge?"

"So?"

"So, after a while, he cooled off and that was that. Now we come to Jonathan Nolan."

"Could you ring bells with him?"

"I could ring bells with you, Lover."

"We were up to Nolan."

"Nolan was my lawyer. A flip guy, and a wise guy, but a shrewdie. He did me a favor once and I don't forget a favor."

"What kind of favor?"

"Two years ago, I was contemplating opening the Club Jolly. I had to buy the building. I had a lot of jack at the time but I didn't have enough. I was short twenty-five thousand bucks. Nolan was always quick with a dollar—to earn it, to spread it, to lend it. He was handling the deal. When this emergency popped up—these things happen in a deal—he advanced the dough. Of course he took back a mortgage and there was interest plus a bonus—but the guy was there with the buck when I needed it and I don't forget."

"Did he get his money back?"

"Within two months. Then later on, he got into trouble, he got disbarred, he went broke, and he sort of passed out of my sphere of things."

"Did he know about Roger's letters?"

"Yeah. We had a giggle about them a few times."

"Let's bring it up to date now, eh?"

"Sure. About three weeks ago, Nolan dropped into the club. He was loaded. He's a trouble guy, a muscle guy. He got into an argument with a customer and he belted him. The guy went back on him and Nolan slugged him with a bottle. That's bad for business, bad for my license. The guy was hustled out and patched up. Nolan wound up in my dressing room where I had him sleep it off."

"Muscle guy," I said. "Sister, that bird is begging for it."

"Every hard guy, sooner or later, catches up with a harder one. It hasn't happened to Nolan yet."

"Hasn't it?" I said.

"Anyway, after a snooze and about a gallon of coffee, he straightened out, and he began to beef to me about how he was broke and how tough things were for him. Then he had a bright idea. I could help him."

"How?"

"That blackmail thing—but without blackmail."

"Now isn't that a cute one! How's it work?"

"He asked me to co-operate. He said I couldn't get into trouble because it wouldn't really be blackmail."

"What would it be—really?"

"A gag that figured to produce some dough—for him."

"How?"

"Like this. I was to get in touch with Roger and pretend I was going to hold him up—just as I did. But I wasn't going through with it. My job was to speak my piece and let it lie there, period. Then, according to Nolan, Roger would come to him, and Nolan would be the hero—for a price. Like that, it wouldn't cost me anything, I'd be returning a favor to a guy who helped me out once— and Nolan would be able to pick up some dough he needed badly."

"Only instead of going to Nolan, Roger came to me."

"So it seems."

"You think he was giving you straight goods?"

"Right now, I don't know. That guy's a deep one. I thought it was straight goods at the time he sprung it. What do you think?"

"I don't know either. But I'm gonna know. Thanks, Anabel. I'm getting out of here."

Her hand came up to my neck and a fingernail scraped gently at my hair. Her eyes were lazy as she tilted her head upward. Softly she said, "What's your hurry, Lover?"

It was rough—but I thought of Aldridge in the can, Root in the morgue and Dodge in the hospital. It was rough—but it would have to keep. I bent down, moved her head away, and kissed the back of her neck. "It'll have to keep," I said, and I stood up.

She looked at me. She didn't move, lying cat-like stretched on the divan, topside down and long and curved and lovely and graceful. Then one leg came up, bent at the knee, long and tapered, waving slowly in the air, the arch of the foot high, the toes pointed. Her lips rounded into the shape of a kiss and one eye closed slowly.

"It'll keep."

I was at the door when she called: "Will you be in touch?"

"Where'll you be?"

"Right here."

"I'll be in touch."

"I'll be waiting."

CHAPTER 12

In the pokey, I talked with Roger Aldridge while Parker hovered nearby. Parker, always the gentlemen, stayed out of earshot. I gave Aldridge the letters and he gave me back an incredulous stare. He read them, re-read them, said, "You're a wizard."

"There are no copies," I said. "What you've got—is all there is."

Aldridge looked toward Parker. "Lieutenant," he called.

"What?" Parker joined us.

"May I have my checkbook, Lieutenant? And a pen?"

Parker's eyes went from him to me, then the eyes narrowed and he smiled, and he sucked at his cheek. "Always making money, these private eyes. Even in jail." He spread his arms at a uniformed officer, bowed, said, "Service, please. Mr. Aldridge's checkbook."

"You kiddin', Lieutenant?"

"I don't kid, young man. I lost whatever was left of my sense of humor when I was promoted to this job."

"Yes, sir, Lieutenant." The young man saluted and departed.

Parker looked at me hard, shrugged, grinned helplessly, and went back to out of earshot, unwrapping a cigar on the way.

Aldridge said, "How'd you get them?"

I brought him up to date.

He said, "You'll destroy them, Mr. Chambers. We can't do it here. Burn them. I know I can depend on you."

"They're as good as burnt right now."

He was silent for a few moments. Then he said: "What do you think Jonathan had in mind?"

"A big touch—and a quick one—for turning up the letters. You offered me fifteen thousand. He might have topped that by ten."

He scratched at his mustache. "I don't know. In a case like this, he wouldn't have left it to chance. Three weeks have already gone by. If he had wanted it—he could have, somehow, arranged it. That occur to you?"

"And how."

"What do you think, then?"

"I don't know. You're the guy that says he uses the rapier rather than the bludgeon. Up to now, it's been strictly bludgeon."

"And completely unlike him."

The man came with the check book and pen. Aldridge wrote a check—to me—for fifteen thousand dollars. I looked at it. I said, "It should be fourteen. You've already paid me one."

"Whose money is it?"

"Yours."

"Let it stand."

You can't hate a guy like that. I put the check away and the letters. I said, "For a guy booked for murder you're taking it real cool."

"I didn't kill him. I've told the truth. I'm not worried. I'm a great believer in the efficiency of the police. They're making a mistake, but they've made mistakes before that have been rectified. But I do wish Warren Dodge had got in touch with me. Have you found him yet?"

The guy had enough worries. I said, "No. But I will."

"Will," he said. "Why in heaven's name should anybody force my uncle to change his will in order to bolster my share?" He brushed a finger at his mustache again, ran the finger up along his cheek and dug it into his temple.

Suddenly, I knew where I was going. I said, "Do you happen to know the phone number of Dodge's secretary? Mamie . . . ?"

"As a matter of fact, I do. Mamie Miller. Lives with her sister. Let me think now." He closed his eyes, remembering, then he gave me the number.

Parker came to us. "Okay," he said. "We break it up now."

Dowstairs, I called Mamie. I asked her to meet me in the lobby of the Flatiron Building, it was important. I hung up and called Jonathan Nolan. He wasn't home.

CHAPTER 13

Mamie took me up to Dodge's office. We put on the lights and I went into the library. I said, "I'm going to do a little studying."

"Studying? Here?" Her face constricted in bewilderment. "Why?"

"Because there's a law library here. I'm playing a hunch. I'm bouncing bludgeons against rapiers, and playing a hunch."

"Hunch?" she said.

"In my business it's part of the standard equipment. Hunch, sixth sense, experience, unconscious urge—it's got a lot of names, and none of them actually makes sense."

"Bludgeons?" she said. "Rapiers?"

"Figures of speech. In a cockeyed kind of way, I'm trying to get the guy that got Mr. Dodge."

That made her decidely happier.

I said, "How is he?"

"I call the hospital each hour, making a real pest of myself. So far, each time, the report is 'Fair.' "

"Could be worse."

"Yes. I'll go outside now and let you work."

I pored over books like a kid giving a workout to pornography. I knew what I was looking for, and I knew where to look, but this wasn't my racket and it took time. I got close a couple of times but not close enough. I checked each reference and the books piled up on the library table like a football heap on an autumn gridiron and then—bang—I had it right on the head. I closed the book and folded it under my arm and went out to Mamie. I said, "Sweetie, we can blow the joint now."

"Blow?" she said. "Joint?"

"I'll take you home. And thanks for the use of the hall. And I'm borrowing this law book."

Dear old Mamie. She said, "Oh. You'll have to sign a receipt." She sat down at the typewriter and tapped out a receipt that had more clauses than Donald Root's will. I signed it and she put out the lights, and we got out of there, and downstairs, I shoved two fingers into my mouth and shrilled for a cab.

I took Mamie home first, and then I had the cabbie drive me to 35th Street, and we stopped at a cafeteria, and he waited while I went in and used a public phone and called Nolan, and got no answer. Mr. Nolan was out having himself a good time, but he wasn't going to have a good time for long. I went back to the cab and said, "10 West 35th."

It turned out to be a four-story house with a remodeled front, an open downstairs door, and no elevators inside. I trudged up two flights to 2 E, rang the bell for just-in-case, and then used Mel's key to invite myself in. I flipped a light and locked the door behind me. I laid down the law book and did quick exploring. There were three rooms:

a bedroom with an extra wide bed; an ample kitchen and a large living room with good furniture, a liquor cabinet with a lot of bottles, and high bookcases along the walls with a preponderance of law books. I moved a chair so that it faced the door, switched off the lights, sat down and let myself get angry.

I didn't smoke. I didn't want him to open door and get a whiff of tobacco. I sat very still and grew rigid, waiting. I thought about a son of a bitch who used a girl for a patsy and put her in a spot where she could do time for attempted extortion. I thought about a burning cigar thrown at the face of a stranger. I thought about a guy grabbing a fallen man's hair and rapping the back of his head against a stone floor. I thought about the back end of a heater crashing into the skull of a man past seventy. I thought about murder, putting a bullet into the head of an invalid trapped in a wheel chair . . . and then there was footfalls in the corridor outside the door, and a key in the lock, and I was standing up, waiting for a guy that was good with his mitts, that had been an amateur champion and a professional pug, a guy with big shoulders and a lot of power and a guy that would stop at nothing.

The door opened and I hit him.

The left caught him in the stomach and he bent over face forward, and the right caught him with all my strength square on the nose, and I could hear the break of bone under the impact of the blow. But he didn't go down. He rushed me and kicked his knee hard to my groin, and I fell against him, and we both fell against the door, closing it. We struggled against the closed door, his knees punching up viciously, always toward my groin. It was too dark to see, but I didn't stop swinging, and then a fist caught me on the point of the chin and I flew back and fell to the floor.

He clicked on the light.

I could see him coming at me now. He plunged forward in a flying leap, and yet, in one second you noticed the craziest things. At the very moment that you saw the blood on his face and his nose blue and twisted, you noticed too that he was wearing the same suit as yesterday, and you saw the watch chain across his vest and the dangling gold boxing glove. He was flying toward me, but the heel of my shoe cracked against his eye and he fell sidewise, and now I was on top of him, a knee in his belly and my fists rapping at his face. But he was strong and somehow, his hands came up and clutched at my throat, and his thumbs pressed in against my Adam's apple, and I wheezed for breath and I fell off him, but I twisted out of the grip of his hands.

He was up now, near the liquor cabinet. He grabbed at the neck of a bottle, smashed off the base against a corner of the cabinet, and he was coming at me, the ragged-edged bottle a murderous weapon. I was on one knee like a runner starting for a sprint. He came at me and I jumped, and I caught the wrist of the hand holding the bottle, and we struggled again, panting, tight to each other, the jagged bottle waving above us, a weapon of many daggers. Sweat popped from both of us, and hand trembled against wrist, and then I swept the hand down and the bottle slashed at his ear, and it slit the ear where it was attached to the head, and the blood came down in a red sheet and it must have frightened him, because the grip on the bottle loosened, and I shook it out of his hand and it fell to the floor, crashing to pieces. He turned just as I wheeled, and my left caught him on the nose again in a full pivot, flat-smashing-soggy-wet, and he stood still like a stricken animal, shaking his head. I had him down to size now. He ripped open his jacket and I saw the holster, and he was fumbling for the gun but he didn't have a chance. It was like chopping down a tree. I kept banging fists at his face as his hands hung loose and he shuddered; then he stumbled and fell flat on his back, spread-eagled and unconscious, blood gurgling from his mouth.

I leaned against a wall and waited for the fire to go out of my lungs. Then I went to him and bent to him and looked at each end of the watch chain and found what I expected. One vest picket held a watch, the other a sharp-bladed gold knife. The knife sparkled clean—Mr. Nolan had done a good job of cleansing it—but nothing was going to help him. I reached into my own pocket for the tuft of red carpet out of Donald Root's apartment. If a clincher was going to be necessary, this would be the clincher. I tucked the tuft deep into the knife pocket, returned the knife, put the watch back in the other pocket, stood up and went to the phone. For the second time in two days I called my doctor in an emergency, but this was some one else's emergency. I got through to him and I said, "Doc?"

"Yes . . . ?"

"Pete Chambers. I need you bad. Emergency."

"Again?"

"Trouble, doc. Can you make it?"

"If it's an emergency . . ."

"It's an emergency. 10 West 35th. Apartment 2 E. As fast as possible. Brother, am I going to get a bill this month."

"Brother, you just said a mouthful.

Nolan slumbered raspingly as I made more phone calls. I called Anabel and I told her to come a-visiting and to come quickly. Then I called Parker at Headquarters. I said, "I've got your murderer."

"Which murderer?"

"Donald Root."

"Wrong number. *I've* got that murderer."

"No you haven't. Come on up here."

"Where?"

"Jonathan Nolan's apartment. 10 West 35th. 2 E."

"That the other nephew?"

"That's right."

"We've been trying to contact him."

"I've got him for you. Reclining and resting. Right here."

"See you, young feller."

"The faster the better. And bring Root's will with you."

"Bye, now."

While I waited I eavesdropped on Roger Aldridge's correspondence. You think of Roger Aldridge, prim with blue-grey temples and a white mustache and an affected enunciation, and you read the incandescent letters that show the man inside the man and it gives you a chuckle.

I built a bonfire in an ashtray and cremated Roger's indiscretions and opened a window and flicked the ashes to oblivion. Then the bell was ringing. It was Doc with his little black bag. He saw his patient at once, opened his bag, and went to work on him. "What happened to this guy?" he muttered. "Get his head caught in a concrete-mixer?"

"Doctors and their corny cracks," I said. "How is he?"

"Pretty bad."

He stitched his eye, took four sutures bringing the ear back to the face, and stuffed plugs into a nostril. He said, "This baby needs a hospital."

"He come to yet?"

"He's semi-conscious." He took a hypo out of his bag.

I said, "What are you going to do?"

"Give him a jab."

"I want him conscious, Doc."

"He'll be conscious but woozy."

"Woozy's all right with me, as long as he stays with us and knows what's going on."

Doc said, "Give me a hand."

We lifted him to a couch and Doc gave him the needle. Then the bell was ringing again, and our first visitor was Anabel Jolly in a mauve suit and glistening nylons and mauve shoes and a black net blouse right up to the neck, and then Parker piled in with a pair of burly cops.

I pointed at the couch. I said, "There's your murderer."

Nolan leaned on one elbow and observed us groggily.

Parker glanced at the patched-up face, and said, "What happened?"

"Concrete-mixer," Doc said.

Parker said, succinctly: "Uh huh."

"The bullet in the ceiling," I said. "That gave it to me right away. I don't care how hard you tried to convince me, Lieutenant, you weren't happy with that bullet in the ceiling."

Parker said, "If you've got a story, let's have it."

"Miss Jolly's got a story first."

"Who's Miss Jolly?"

"The lady in the purple suit. You've got the floor, Anabel."

Miss Jolly told her story.

"That," said Parker, "implicates him in a blackmail deal. It doesn't make him out a murderer. He was looking for a big touch and a fast one."

"Wrong," I said.

"Why?"

"Because this guy was looking for more than two hundred and fifty thousand dollars. He was reaching for the jackpot. Plus."

"Plus?" Parker said. "Plus what?"

"Plus your way—that does it with a bludgeon." I shook my head. "Not this baby. This one makes with a rapier."

Parker squinted his eyes. "What? What's that?"

"This guy's complex, a brain-guy. The blackmail deal was to provide a motive for Roger Aldridge. Exactly what you fell for. All of a sudden, Aldridge needed two hundred and fifty thousand dollars. And he needed it bad. A partnership in Winston Parnell was at stake."

"Let's have the story," Parker said. "*Your* way."

"Nolan knew that Aldridge didn't have that kind of loot. He knew that sooner or later he'd appeal to Donald Root. So he kept an eye on him and today, when Aldridge finally went to Root, Nolan was his tail. He had this on him." I went to Nolan, opened his jacket, took the gun out of the holster and gave it to Parker. "Exhibit One," I said.

Parker fondled the gun. "Go on."

"Nolan knew that Emerson Beach was off. He knew that Beach was due back at five. Nolan is a nephew—he knew all about the old man's habits. So . . . as close to five as he dared, he rang the bell, ducked when Aldridge answered, then jumped him and blasted him with the butt end of the heater."

"That way," Parker said, "going along with your story, Aldridge couldn't identify his assailant."

"Correct. He knew that Aldridge carried a gun. We'll suppose, of course, he wore gloves. He took out Aldridge's gun, threatened the old man, got the will out of the safe where it was kept and had the old man change it . . . under threat of death. This done, he plugged the old man. With Aldridge's gun. Then he put the gun in Aldridge's hand and shot another bullet. The one in the ceiling."

This time it was Doc who asked the question. "Why?"

"To get cordite impregnations in Aldridge's hand. These show up in a thing called the paraffin gauntlet test. The Lieutenant understands."

Parker said, "Yeah."

"Then he turned him around to face the door, as though he were on his way out. Then he cut a slit in the carpet to make it look as though it had torn when Aldridge supposedly tripped on it. Then he scuffed it wide with the point of Aldridge's shoe, stuck the point in, and now it looked like Aldridge tripped and knocked himself out in his hurry to scram. He had to work fast. He wanted Aldridge still unconscious when Beach returned."

"Any ideas," Parker said, "as to what he used to cut this alleged slit?"

I went near to Nolan. "He wears this watch chain." I reached in for the knife attached to the chain. "This, Lieutenant, is a knife. And it looks like it's recently been cleaned." I dug into the pocket, and then, surprise, surprise, I came up with a tuft of red carpet. "But I think, Lieutenant, that he forgot to clean the pocket."

This was evidence. The Lieutenant alerted to action. He grabbed the tuft of carpet, examined it, took a piece of paper out of his pocket, folded it into the paper and put the paper away. "Anthing else?" he said.

"Plenty else. He was through, and he wanted to get out fast, away from the scene of action. He had rigged his plant and he wanted out. He knew nothing of the fact that I was due there and Warren Dodge. He knew Beach was due and he wanted to duck out. But as the elevator came down, he saw Warren Dodge in the lobby. Dodge had his back to him. It wouldn't do for Dodge to see him there, it wouldn't do at all. So out came the heater, and he opened Dodge's skull with it. It took eleven stitches to close it."

"Where's Dodge now?"

"You're Homicide. You wouldn't know."

"What does that mean?"

"Means that you don't know about every single police inquiry in the city. Dodge is at the Flower Hospital . . . and he's sort of held out a bit of information on the cops. But the minute you fix him up with the facts, you'll have his full statement."

"Question, please."

"You say his back was turned." He jerked his thumb at Nolan. "Then how'd he see this guy?"

"He was facing a mirror. He saw him but he couldn't get out of the way in time. That's positive evidence, Lieutenant."

To Nolan, Parker said, "Can you talk?"

"I can talk," Nolan said.

"Any remarks?"

"Strictly a frame."

Grimly, Parker said, "It's a frame you're going to punch hard to get out of."

"Where's motive?" Nolan said. "I wouldn't kill Root to make Roger richer. You may be able to hold me, Lieutenant, but a jury'll throw you out of court."

Parker twisted to me. "He's got a point there."

"No he hasn't."

"Why?"

"Because I can show you motive. This is a shrewdie. He works boths ends against the middle. It only *looks* like no motive."

"Show me," Parker said.

"You know that Nolan is the only heir-at-law of Donald Root. The only one beside the guy you've got in the clink."

"So?"

"Where's the will?"

Parker produced it.

"Notice," I said, "that the additional bequest is written *after* the signature."

"I also notice that the bequest is to Roger Aldridge, not Jonathan Nolan. Where's the percentage?"

"Hold it," I said. I strode to the law book, real legal-counsel-courtroom-manner, and opened it to the place I had marked. "My reference," I said in my best lawyer-like tones, "is to a case entitled In Re Ryan's Will, 252 N.Y. 620. Therein we have a rule of law. *A will is void when not signed at its physical end.* Thus, if after the signature, there is more writing of a dispository nature, the will is not signed at its physical end, and it is therefore void in its entirety. That's the law, Lieutenant."

The Lieutenant scratched his head. "Sure," he said. "If the will is void, Donald Root dies intestate. Intestate—which means without a will—then his heirs-at-law inherit. That cuts Nolan in for half the estate."

"Very good, Lieutenant." I snapped the book shut.

The Lieutenant beckoned one of the police officers. "Nippers," he remarked in his most acidly courteous manner, "for Mr. Nolan."

The officer grinned and complied. Jonathan Nolan was finished and he looked it. I wasn't.

"Just in case that wouldn't work," I said, "there's another rule of law."

Parker beamed. "Hidden talents," he said. "A real legal eagle."

"There's a rule of law that states that a criminal cannot profit by his wrongdoing. Thus, if Nolan's plant worked, Aldridge would be convicted of the murder . . . which covered Nolan two ways. First, if the will were declared void, then the entire estate would go to the heirs. Since Aldridge could not profit by his own wrongdoing . . . the entire estate would go to one Jonathan Nolan."

"And second?" Parker said.

"If, by chance, the will would hold up—"

"How?" Parker said.

"There are lawyers and lawyers, and the law's got more curves than . . . than . . . even Anabel Jolly."

Demurely, Miss Jolly said, "Thanks. Lots."

"Anyway, if it did hold up, then the charitable bequest would go to the charity named—but, once again, Aldridge's share could not go to Aldridge—same reason—criminal cannot profit by his own wrongdoing. Then—what would happen?"

"What?" said Miss Jolly, her eyes wide now, her red mouth puckered in the beginning of a small smile. "Terrific, this boy, isn't he?" Now the smile was big and beaming.

"If you'll look, Lieutenant, you'll see there's no residual clause in the will, no direction as to what happens with any part of the estate that, for some reason, cannot go as the testator wished. For that share of the estate, then, the testator, Donald Root is deemed to have no will. And his heir-at-law inherits. Who dat? Jonathan Nolan again."

"So the worst that could happen to him," Parker said, "is that he winds up with half the estate, which would be—from what our investigation shows—at least half a million, maybe plenty more."

"How's that for motive?"

"Pretty good," Parker acknowledged. "And pretty slick."

"Finished?" inquired Anabel Jolly.

"All done," I said.

"Put the book away."

I put the book away.

She took me under the arm and led me to the door.

Parker called: "I need this guy."

"Not more than I do," Jolly called back. She smiled, winked, composed her face to elfish innocence. "I'll save some of him. Got some cross-examining of my own to do."

"Cross-examining?" Parker said.

"He's good at making like a detective, and he's good at talking like a lawyer. I'm curious to discover how good he is at ringing bells."

"Bells?" said Parker.

"Bells, Lieutenant."

She opened the door and marched me out.

11

LOOSE END

You think, sometimes, philosophically.

You think of wars that were and wars to come and big wars and little wars and so-called comic opera wars, and you think about the human beings that were involved in all of them, and you know that to each of these, no matter, it was a big war, an immense war, a gigantic war—because he was in it—it was personal to every one of them and soul-consuming and all-out distracting and big and important as life itself—and I hear tell that life is considered important. Bring it down to tiny things. Bring it down to a nose. You've got a nose and it's natural to breathe through it, and who thinks about having a nose; but you get yourself an ingrown hair, you get yourself an inside blown-up boil, and it sounds like a laugh to the next guy—but brother, all of a sudden, it's just not a nose like everybody's got a nose—all of a sudden it's big, vast, and hurting-important—all of a sudden there are doctors probing and shaking their heads and telling you how near the brain it is—and all of a sudden you can die from it—and it's big, then, isn't it?—it's vast, big, personal, devastatingly-near-to-death important.

Because it's your nose.

And wars are like that, if it's your war.

I'll never forget that kid, straight and serious, moving there opposite me, up and back like a caged animal, a boy thrown up at the tail end of a little war—police action it was called—a kid whose face had a strange look of wax.

He was tall and thin and intent and he kept filling my ashtray with cigarette butts. His face was sunburnt but the look of wax came through. It was an old face for a young man; there were anguish lines, and the eyes were tired and careless.

He paced in front of my desk, ground out the cigarette and lit a new one. He used the same hand for lighting the cigarette as he did for placing it between his lips. He had no other hand. The sleeve of his blue suit was in the pocket of his jacket, and it was empty all the way down from the shoulder. He said, "I came to you because I'd heard about you. Been hearing about you for a long time."

I said, "Thanks."

He said, "I got no dough."

I said, "Let's not talk about dough. Yet."

He came near and he sat down in the chair facing me and he grinned. "I've been here fifteen minutes maybe twenty, and we haven't said a thing to each other, I mean anything real, have we?"

"Smoked a lot of cigarettes for fifteen minutes. I'd say it's nearer an hour that you've been here."

"An hour?" The grin was wider, and young, but the eyes stayed old. "Maybe you're good company, Mr. Chambers. Maybe I am. But you don't know yet why I'm here."

"I'm in no hurry. We've chatted. I know things about you. I know your name is Casey Moore."

"And that I'm holed up at the Montero on upper Broadway."

"And that you were in a prison camp for two years and were returned with the truce. I know that you were here in a hospital in the States for four months. And I certainly know more about Commie prison camps than I knew before we had out chat."

"Yeah," he said. "And you know that I've got no left arm and a lot of my belly ain't where it used to be . . . but you don't know what brings me to a private detective."

"Not yet I don't."

"I repeat I've got no dough."

"I heard you the first time, Casey."

"And I don't want charity, either. I'm not trading on a war record."

"Save that, Casey, huh? Let's get the story first. Let's worry about the dough when we get up to that."

He pushed his hand across his mouth. "You . . . you're a nice guy. You're cracked up to be a tough one, real tough. I don't know." The grin came again. "I think you're a softie."

"Think so myself." I shrugged. "Of course, there are people who'll disagree with that. But what the hell. There are people who'll disagree with anything. Let's have the story."

"There ain't much, really."

"Okay. Let's have what you've got."

He sighed. Long, deep and whistling. From all the way down. Then he said, "There was me and there was my old man and there was nobody else. My mother died when I was a baby. The old man brought me up."

"What's his name?"

"Henry. Henry Moore. We lived out in Queens, out by the edge of Flushing. A little wooden house in Queens. That's where I was raised." The lids came down on his eyes and he looked past me in reminiscence. "Great guy, the old man. Dreamer-type guy. Used to paint pictures. Had them all over the walls of the house. Everybody thought they stank. Except me. And him. I thought they were beautiful."

"What'd he do for a living?"

"Bank guard. That's the best picture my mind makes. The old man in a light blue uniform with a Sam Browne belt and a gun in a holster. Never used that gun in twenty years, as it happens. Directed ladies to the right window, helped old guys make out withdrawal slips, changed up the pen points in the pens . . . worked that bank twenty years, all branches, never had one minute of excitement.

"He still there?"

His face clouded."No."

"Retired?"

"Let me tell you."

"Sorry."

"He never saved a sou, spent it on me, mostly. He insisted I get an education. I was always a bug on flying. I got my degree out of Columbia and I learned all they could teach me about aeronautics. Went to flying school too. Then I got a job as pilot on one of the airlines, pushed one of the big ones, transcontinental."

"And your dad?"

"Arthritis was plaguing him. Don't get me wrong, Mr. Chambers, he wasn't an old man. He was fifty. But I was earning enough for the two of us now, so I talked him into it. He retired."

I reached across for one of his cigarettes and lit up.

"Then what?"

"Then I got drafted into that Korean mess."

"And then?"

"I went over as a bomber pilot."

"Your father stay retired?"

"No. He took a part-time job as a night watchman. Worked three days a week." He got up and started pacing again. "The Korean thing went quick for me. We got shot down early right after the Chinese moved in. Twelfth mission they got us. Two of us were flung clear, and then the thing blasted like a fire rocket. I learned later the whole crew was listed as dead, including me.

"How about the guy that was flung clear with you?"

"We were picked up by an enemy patrol. He died on the march back. I don't know how I made it but seems I did. They took off what was left of my arm, pushed my belly together and sewed it up, but I made it. And I made it through the years at the prisoner of war camp."

"Yeah," I said. I dumped the cigarette. "Then the truce, and the four months here in the hospital. I bet the happiest man in the world was your dad."

He stopped walking, and turned his back to me. I could see his shoulders hunch. He said, "I didn't hear from him. Not a word."

"Come again?"

"Not a word. I was informed that he couldn't be found." Now he turned and came back to me and he leaned his one hand on the desk and bent toward me. Something stirred in his old eyes. "Four months of rehabilitation and then two days ago, the day of discharge, they told me. One of the top medics called me into his office and told me."

"Told you what?"

"That my father was dead. That he had been killed during the committing of a crime, a burglary, of which he was the perpetrator."

What do you say to that? What do you say to a boy with one arm and part of a stomach and tired eyes and an old face marred by anguish lines? What do you say to a kid bent over your desk, jaw muscles working in a sunburnt face, the strange look of wax coming through, the pallor that won't stay hidden by the burn of the sun, pallor of years in a prison camp, a kid without an arm and a hole in his stomach? What do you say to him?

You say nothing. You sit still and you stare up at him and you wait.

The hand came off my desk and he straightened. He went away, walked about the room, came back and slumped into the chair facing me. He said, "They made it easy for me. They gave me an old newspaper clipping." He fished in his pocket, brought out the clipping and handed it across. I watched him light a cigarette and then I went to work on the clipping.

It was dated a year ago, May 11th. It told of an attempted burglary at the Westchester home of one Edward Adams. The attempt had been made at two o'clock in the morning. The intruder, one Henry Moore, had entered by the front door. The lady of the house, Dorothy Adams, had heard a noise, had called to her husband, and then without waiting, had gone to investigate. The intruder, in panic, had emptied a gun at her. Edward Adams, who had stopped to take his own gun out of a drawer, a gun for which he had a proper license, had quickly followed his wife and had, in turn, emptied his gun at the intruder, killing him. A person by the name of Matthew Bennett, a house guest, had awakened, and had been a witness to the latter part of the proceedings. Henry Moore had once been a bank guard and the gun he used belonged to him. Mrs. Dorothy Adams had been critically wounded. The police had been called and a doctor, who had attended her, but she had expired before she could be taken to a hospital. Henry Moore resided at 116 Whitehall Place, Flushing, Queens.

There was a curious last paragraph to the clipping. Earlier that evening, at eleven o'clock, Henry Moore's home in Queens had been burnt to the ground. The fire had broken out in four of the seven rooms of the wooden edifice and was "undoubtedly of incendiary origin."

I finished and leaned back.

Casey Moore said, "Nice, huh?"

I didn't say anythingthing. I returned the clipping.

Casey Moore said, "Impossible. Absolutely crazy. It couldn't happen."

"What have you done about it?"

"Couldn't happen," he said. "Nobody can talk me into it. I knew my old man. I loved the guy. It . . . it must have been someone else."

"Think so, Casey?"

He shook his head slowly. "No."

"What have you done? Up to now?"

"Went to the cops. To find out. To get squared away on this thing." His voice moved up a notch. "No question. It was my father."

"Whom did you speak to there?"

"A Captain Weaver at Police Headquarters. I saw photographs, everything. I told him it couldn't happen, not my father, it couldn't happen, something was wrong, something was crazy . . ." His voice dribbled out. He was silent, staring, looking at the blank wall over my head. Then he said: "Captain Weaver was a nice man. He was kind and sympathetic. But he said it *did* happen, that the proof was all in, that the case was closed, and that one way or another, my father was dead, and why didn't I leave it alone?"

I pushed back out of my swivel chair, stood up, stretched my legs, went to the window and looked out on the many people scurrying along the New York street. It was a warm spring day, one of the best kind of days in the city. The sun was a dappled yellow blanket, there was a soft breeze, and the colors of the city were bright and clear. I kept looking out the window, the breeze on my face. I said, "What do you want me to do, Casey?"

He said, "Two years in a prison camp. It's a lifetime."

I said nothing.

"You get old like that," he said. "You think old. Things come into perspective. You've got a lot of time to think. You grow up, you're not a boy any more."

"What do you want me to do, Casey?"

"Things come into perspective; the virtues you toss off as corny when you're a boy. Love, honor, respect, integrity, stuff like that." He rose and came near me at the window. "My father's dead. But he's dead as a murderer. That's dreadfully wrong. And it's important to me to prove that it's wrong. Can you understand that, Mr. Chambers?"

"Yes."

"That's what I want you to do for me. The police won't—because for them it's over. The proof is perfect and the case is closed. All they've got now is me ranting that it couldn't happen. I suppose every son thinks it can't happen to his father."

"Casey."

"Yes?"

"What makes you think I won't agree with the concept of the police?"

"I don't think anything. I'm appealing to you. I tell you my father was not a thief and he was not a murderer. I tell you that and you must believe me. I want you to prove that. Prove that for me."

"And if I can't? If it's impossible?"

"Then at least I know I tried. And I don't want you to work for nothing. I have no money now, no real money, But after you're through—win, lose or draw—you'll send me your bill and I'll pay it, if it takes me a couple of years to pay it."

"Forget that bill stuff, will you, Casey?"

"But—"

"For now, forget it." I moved away from the window. I reached for his pack on the desk, gave him a cigarette and took one for myself. I was about to offer him a light but thought the better of it. I lit mine. He lit his. I said, "Henry Moore. You say he couldn't steal."

"That's right. It wasn't in him."

"Could he kill?"

Smoke flickered from his nostrils. He was quiet a moment, thinking. He said, "My father would be capable of killing . . . in self-defense, perhaps." Silence again, then: "And, I believe, in one other case. Euthanasia."

"Youth and *what?*"

"Mercy killing. He was bugged on the subject. Talked about it often. For instance, if I, his son, were incurably ill and in pain, and the doctors said there was absolutely no hope, my father believed that someone like that, even if it were his own son or himself should be put out of his misery."

"I'm not talking about that. I mean, killing, putting a gun to a human being and pumping bullets. Like what happened to Mrs. Adams."

"He couldn't do it. Absolutely not. He couldn't have broken into a house, and murdered a strange woman."

"But he did, didn't he? The police aren't crazy. According to you, they had it foursquare, and it's stacked away as closed."

"Sure. That's the way it looked, and maybe . . . maybe that's the way it was. But I won't believe it. I want it checked again. By you. From the beginning. I'd do it myself, if I knew how. Will you give it a try, Mr. Chambers? Will you, sir? Please?"

"Yes, I will."

"Thank you."

"Forget it."

"And now . . . is there anything *I* can do to help?"

"You can go on about your business, and don't broadcast that you're around the town. And don't talk about this to anyone. I know where I can reach you and I'll report to you—as you put it—win, lose or draw. Fair enough?"

"The best."

I took him to the door. I said, "Good-bye, lad. I'll be in touch."

Caper, they call it. When a private detective goes to work on a case they call it a caper. I once looked it up in a dictionary. It means: "a playful leap or spring, a prank." Well, how do you go about leaping and springing on a matter like this? Where do you begin on a playful little springing prank that already involves arson, burglary, and two violent deaths?

You start by walking the office carpet and you scratch

your head. You think of a kid with old eyes and faith in his father and you wonder whether it isn't just that: faith—splendid and soul-deep and unswerving, but hopeless against the impersonal logic of the law. You think of a father who went all the way out for a kid, who brought him up strong, who lost him to a cockpit over fighting armies; and then you think of a kid who comes back out of the dead to find his father branded a thief and a murderer; and you hope with all the miserable hope that is in you that you can do something for him. You kick once at the carpet, march through to the outer office, slam on a hat, wave to your secretary, and you go to the source. You go to Police Headquarters.

Captain Edgar Weaver was a detective out of Homicide, practiced in his profession for thirty years. He was bald and thin with black lashes around white-gray uncompromising eyes: when he turned them up at you they hit like sudden headlights out of the dark. Weaver gave a man his due—plain citizen, incorrigible hood, suspected murderer, or private detective. He said, "What do you figure to do that cops can't do? Or haven't done?"

"I don't know," I said. "But I want to do whatever I can to give that kid a break."

"That's an excellent notion. But I repeat—it's open and shut. So how are you going to change it?"

"Open and shut—that way you don't have to dig too hard."

"You can't dig when you've hit bottom, Mr. Peeper. That file is sitting there right in front of you."

"File," I said. I looked at it a bit. Then I said, "How come you people have a file on it? It happened up there in Westchester. Mamaroneck. That's not New York City business."

"No, but Henry Moore was a Queens resident. That's New York City business. We were called in, and we've got duplicates of everything in the Westchester file."

"The cops there satisfied?"

"Perfectly. Plus the Coronet Insurance Company paid out two hundred thousand dollars. The woman was insured for a hundred with double indemnity for accidental death. They paid the double indemnity in full. So you see you've really got it stacked against you, Mr. Peeper. You've got cops satisfied, *and* an insurance company satisfied. You think you can break that down?"

"Tell you the truth, I don't. But I'd like to give it a whirl."

"I've got nothing against that."

"Anything you can tell me on it?"

"You've got the file in front of you."

"Files make me dizzy. Any angles?"

His grey eyes shot up at me. "One. The guy didn't have to break in. The front door was open."

"Any explanation?"

"Well, Mr. Edward Adams got home about an hour before the attempted burglary. He had been in New York. Maybe he was a little tanked up. Maybe he left it open. He has no recollection on it."

"Happens. But how'd the cops know that door was open?"

"Because there was no forced entry and the dead man had no key to the premises on his person."

I glanced down at the file again. I said, "Two hundred thousand dollars. That's a lot of potatoes. Who's this Edward Adams?"

"Owns the Stardust Room over in Jersey."

"*That* Eddie Adams?"

"You know him?"

"Never actually met him but I've heard enough about him, and I know that Stardust Room, know it well. Beautiful joint."

"Only opened about six months ago, and it took them six months before that to build it. Eddie Adams and a partner, Jack Rawlings."

"Don't know him either. But I know the manager of the place, Matt—." I grabbed at the file again, read one of the sheets and put it down. "Anything smell, Captain?"

"Like what?"

"Like Matt Bennett being the witness?"

"Might, except for Mrs. Adams' statement. She gave the Westchester police a full statement before she died. Coincided exactly with the facts as given both by Adams and Bennett."

"Yeah," I said. "Yeah." I brought out a cigarette and put fire to it. "How old is this Eddie Adams now?"

"Sixty-three. Playboy type. Has been all his life."

"And the wife, Dorothy Adams?"

"She was sixty when she died. That's a year ago. remember."

"Any one of them have the acquaintance of this Henry Moore?"

"Not a one. Complete stranger. You got the statements right there in front of you. And you got a statement there from a Robert Crawford that sort of fixes the whereabouts of Henry Moore that day. Actual date is May 10th. Happened at two o'clock that night, which makes it May 11th. Take a look at that statement."

I looked.

Robert Crawford owned a roadside motel and tavern in Mamaroneck near the Adams home. A man, since identified as Henry Moore, had checked into the motel at six o'clock of the evening of May 10th. He had retired to his room with no baggage. He came out again at about midnight, had a few drinks and a meal, lingered over another few drinks until about one-forty-five, and then left. He never returned. The next day, after the attempted burglary and the shootings, Robert Crawford saw a picture of him in the local newspaper, and identified the body in the morgue as the person who had been his recent lodger.

"Satisfied?" Captain Weaver said.

"Certainly puts him at the scene of the crime. What about that other thing?"

"What other thing?"

"The house that burnt down. Henry Moore's. That happened at eleven on the evening of the same May 10th."

"Burned. Period. A wooden firetrap. Burned all the way down, and everything in it that was burnable."

"Any dope on that?"

"Somebody put the torch to it, no question. Maybe an enemy, maybe vandals, maybe crazy kids." Weaver closed his eyes and leaned back. "Not much for you to go on, is there?"

"No, sir, there ain't."

"It's open and shut, Chambers. Open and shut."

"You don't mind if I nose around on it anyway?"

"Not at all. That's a nice kid, that Casey Moore." His eyes opened and he came forward in his chair. "Call me if anything pops."

"Eddie Adams." I collected my hat and went to the door. "That's a guy with a lot of loot."

"They all have their ups and downs."

"He used to own the Diamond Circle, didn't he?"

"That's the guy but that joint folded."

"Stardust Room's a bang-up success though."

"Couldn't last a day in New York. It's in the municipality of Lake Manor. Local government covers it and those babies cover local government. By those babies, I mean Eddie Adams."

"He still live up there in Mamaroneck?"

"No. He's nearer our bailiwick now. Moved to an estate out at Lido." He reached across his desk for the file, pulled it to him, closed it and spread his hands across the cover. "That's it, Mr. Peeper. It's my hunch you're banging your head against a wall. You figure to bounce off bruised. Maybe

I'm wrong. I've been wrong before. Good-bye and keep in touch. Have fun."

I called the office for messages but there were no messages because the office was closed. I checked the time: it was six o'clock. I came out of the phone booth and into the air and I breathed deep of the soot of springtime in New York. I had time to kill. I had nothing to do until at least eleven o'clock. I took a cab up to 46th Street and had a meal of Mexican food. I practiced my Spanish with the waiter, paid, went out and walked home. Home is 59th Street off Sixth Avenue which is Central Park South when you wish to be impressive. The pall of twilight was descending. Twilight. Romantic word. Twilight can mean the setting of a red ball of sun, the haze of sweet-smelling dusk, distant mountains folding into vapor, the hypnotic aroma of flowers going to sleep: the soft, restful, fragile, precariously beautiful moment of pause as the long day merges into night. Not in New York. In New York, twilight is dirty; there is the smell of gasoline exhaust, the honking of horns, the rumble of buses, the screech of brakes, the gutters clogged, the streets black with the hurrying people, the shift from day to night, the break from work-time to play-time, the eight million souls doing the switch, the feeding of eight million mouths, the fury accelerating, the people of the night beginning to come alive. Eight million people clustered on a pinpoint of the universe, each an individual enclosed in his own thoughts and wrapped in his own desires; and one, without an arm and with a crevice in his stomach, holed up somewhere in a second-rate hotel on upper Broadway, eating his heart out because he came back from the dead to be slapped by the shock of an incredible incident, fresh to him but ancient to the rest of us, already a year old and a closed item in a musty file.

I went home and I showered and shaved. I tried to nap but I couldn't sleep. I watched a night baseball game on television and sipped beer from the cans. Then I dressed carefully, in a blue suit, black shoes, white shirt and dark tie. I thought about wearing a holster and gun but rejected that. I put out the lights, locked up and walked across to Eighth Avenue where my garage was located. I don't often use my car. There are traffic problems in New York and parking problems. But I was going out of New York. I was going to Jersey, to the town of Lake Manor, the chief industry of which was a night club called the Stardust Room.

It was only six months in existence, the Stardust Room, but already it was the most notorious trap on the East Coast. It was a small but beautiful establishment built at a reputed cost of a half million dollars. The entertainment was the best and most exclusive in the land, the food superb, the service obsequious, the music distinguished, and the soft lighting and intimate décor could convert a left-handed lady tugboat queen to a glamour doll with poise. The Stardust Room had most of the qualifications necessary for the assured success of a night club but it had added one more. Within two months of its opening, word wafted over to the big town that if you had a taste for gambling and decried the furtive hush-hush of the usual floating crap games, you didn't have to journey to Las Vegas: the basement rooms of the Stardust were running lush and wide open. There had been a change in the political administration of the town of Lake Manor—and the wise boys had moved in. It was a half hour's ride from midtown Manhattan through the Lincoln Tunnel. I had been there several times before, but this was the first time I was going on business.

I turned the car over to the parking attendant, crunched across on gravel and walked up six marble steps into the wide anteroom that housed the bar. I ordered Scotch and water and looked across the bar into the room proper. It was going full blast, crowded with dancing couples in evening clothes.

"Busy," I said to the bartender.

"Never let's up here."

"Matt Bennett around?"

"Who's asking?"

"Peter Chambers."

His smile was more sneer than smile. "Who's Peter Chambers?"

"Me."

"Who're you?"

"Peter Chambers."

"Who's that?"

"Friend of Matt's."

Unenthusiastically, he said, "Don't mind if I check that, do you?"

"I wish you would."

The smile stayed on his face as he looked me over, then he lifted a phone from a hook attached to the inner part of the bar. He talked into it but I couldn't hear him. Then he hooked the phone back and now his smile had more respect. "He's in his office, Mr. Chambers. You know where it is?"

"Yes." I paid my bar tab and left no tip. That finally killed his smile.

To the left of the long bar was a carpeted stairway going

down. The office of The Manager was at the foot of the stairs. I knocked on the door and it was opened by a slender man with a broken nose. He had a white scar over one eyebrow and squinting eyes like blue agates. He took one look at me, put a fist against my chest and shoved.

"Out," he said.

I flicked off the fist and closed the door behind me. I said, "Remember me, Frankie?"

"I remember you, fink. Too good I remember you."

Frankie Gold was a brainless hoodlum who was quick with a gun. Like every brainless hoodlum he was used as a hatchet man or bodyguard. It had been my pleasure, at one time, to be instrumental in removing Frankie Gold from his usual haunts for a period of two years, time off for good behavior. Now Frankie Gold put his hand within the jacket of his tuxedo and showed me his gun. His scarred eyebrow twitched.

"Out," he said. "Quick."

"I want to see Matt."

"You ain't going to see nobody."

"He's expecting me."

The agate eyes took on an uncomprehending look. "You talking straight?"

"I always talk straight," I said sweetly.

His eyes shifted from me to a black polished door at the far end of the room, then back to me. I could have taken his gun away from him right then but I saw no sense in ruffling myself or him, merely for the purpose of making an impression. I had already made an impression on Frankie Gold. I said, "Put away the heater and go knock on the door."

He hesitated.

"Go on, Frankie. Move it."

He hesitated another moment, then, sullenly, he put his gun back and went to the polished door. He knocked and Matt's deep voice came:

"What is it?"

"Guy out here to see you. A fink by name Chambers."

"Okay."

Matt Bennett opened the door. I bowed to Frankie, pushed him out of the way, and followed Matt into the office.

Matt Bennett was another type of hoodlum. Matt Bennett had brains, polish, culture and the conscience of a curled-up snail. He flipped the door shut and stuck out his hand.

"Hi," he said. "How's business?"

We shook hands and he went to the chair behind his desk and sat heavily. Matt Bennett was a big man. I'm six feet two but Matt was inches taller than I, with bruiser's shoulders and the beginning of a paunch in the middle. He had a square face and black hair and wide black innocent eyes. Matt had been a lawyer once but had been disbarred early in his career. Thereafter it had been the chase for the easy buck, and Matt had made it big. He had been connected with Eddie Adams at the Diamond Circle, and now he was manager in charge of the Stardust Room.

"If you want to cash a check," he said, "the sky's the limit for you."

"No check, Matt. Business."

"Anything I can do for you, pal. Any time."

I jerked a thumb over my shoulder. "That's a new boy you've got outside?"

"Yeah. Know him?"

"Knew him once. A little gun-happy, I'd say."

He frowned at that, seriously. "So I've been told and I'm trying to talk him out of that. Very efficient, otherwise." He smiled with shiny capped teeth. "What's the business, pal?"

"I'd like to talk with Eddie Adams."

"Can't do. He's away."

"Can I get to him?"

"Nope. Little vacation, sort of. On his yacht. Pleasure trip. Little vacation with a couple of close friends."

"When's he due back?"

He shrugged. "Search me. Any time. Maybe quick, maybe a long time. Something I can do?"

"Maybe."

"Shoot, pal. I got a lot of respect for you. You know that."

I slid into an easy chair, slumped, lit a cigarette. "I'm working on a thing, Matt, ties up with another thing. A thing you were in on once."

"Me?"

"Yeah. The night Mrs. Dorothy Adams was killed."

I watched him. Nothing happened. He merely looked quizzical. He said, "What do you mean *I* was in on that?"

"You were there, weren't you?"

"Sure I was. But I wasn't *in* on anything. The old dame got it and got it bad. But that's old stuff, fella. What's the production on it now?"

"Can I ask about the facts?"

"Why not? Nothing I can tell you that I didn't already tell the cops."

"Okay. First off, what were you doing up there?"

"House guest."

"How come?"

He stood up. "Let me get you a drink."

"No, thanks."

He went to a small bar, poured whiskey into a highball glass, added ice and a squirt of seltzer and sat in a chair near me. "Eddie Adams' wife was sick. Lung trouble, asthma, something, I don't know. That was about the time the Diamond Circle folded. Eddie had to be in town late, working over books or something. Anyway, he called me, told me his wife wasn't feeling too hot, and would I go up there and spend the day since he figured to come home pretty late."

"That's all?,"

"That's all, so help me."

"Would you tell me the rest of it?"

"Sure, pal. I went up there—he had his place in Mamaroneck at that time. I had nothing else to do anyway, since the Circle had folded. I spent the day up there, turned in early about ten o'clock. Then about two o'clock that shooting started. It woke me, and I ran out."

"Would you give me the setup of the house?"

"Living rooms, kitchens and stuff, downstairs. Bedrooms upstairs. Eddie and his wife were in one bedroom. My bedroom was opposite theirs on the other side of the stairway. The shooting woke me. Mrs. Adams was at the top of the stairs and this guy was pouring it on from the foot of the stairs. Then Eddie came tearing out and shot up the bum downstairs. That's it, period."

"Thanks."

Ice jiggled as he drank. He wiped his mouth with the back of his hand. "What are you working on, pal?"

"I wish I could tell you, Matt."

"Confidential?"

"You know how it is."

"You could have gone to the cops for this information."

"I like my information firsthand." I stood up and stubbed out my cigarette. "Thanks, Matt. One favor."

"You call it."

"Don't mention to Mr. Adams that I inquired about this."

He put his drink away. "Why not?"

"I wouldn't like him to think I'm prying into his affairs. With others, that is. I'll be talking to him, personally, when he gets back. So you keep it under your hat. Okay, Matt?"

He smiled, his innocent eyes crinkling. "Promise," he said, and he exaggerated making a cross over his heart.

"I'm serious, Matt."

"I promised, didn't I?"

"Fine. And now I'll take you up on that check-cashing deal."

"Going to give the basement a whirl?"

"I'm going to try."

I wrote a check and he went to a large safe, opened it and counted out the money. "If you're going to play the dice," he said, "play them wrong. They've been cold all night."

"Thanks, Matt. By the way, Adams had a partner here, didn't he?"

"Yeah. When they opened. Jack Rawlings. But they split up. Adams is sole owner now. Here's your dough, pal. And play them wrong."

I got back to town at four-thirty in the morning. I was a hundred and twelve dollars richer, but I hadn't learned a thing that would be of any help to Casey Moore. I'm an old hand at asking questions. Matt Bennett hadn't been lying. He hadn't held back a thing. Matt was a wise owl. He could have balked at the answers if there was anything to balk at. But he had given them to me straight and without any hesitation. It added up tight and without any leakage—the police had a closed file, the insurance company had turned over two hundred thousand dollars, and Matt Bennett had been cordial and cooperative. Couldn't be worse for Casey Moore. But I was thinking as a normal human being. The criminal mind thinks differently. The criminal mind is always one jump ahead of the normal mind: cops figure this in advance. So do private investigators. It's one of the reasons they go about asking questions. They are stirring up the criminal mind.

I was hoping.

I parked my car alongside the curb on the south end of Central Park, and went across to my apartment house. The doorman was more solicitous than he had ever been. He opened the door for me, smiled, scraped, bowed, and walked me all the way back to the elevators. Doormen come awake prior to Christmas, but this was spring and it was half past four in the morning. I punched the button for the elevator and the doorman coughed. He had hoped, I trust, for a discreet cough. It came up like a long rumble out of a giraffe.

I said, "What's the matter, Louis?"

He said, "Mr. Chambers, sir . . ."

I said, "Louis, if you're looking for a touch, you got me at the right moment. How much and when do I get it back?"

"No, sir," he said, "it ain't that."
"What is it, Louis?"
"It's . . . it's I can pick up twenty bucks."
"Pick away, Louis. Who am I to gainsay you?"
"Gainsay?" he said.
"Skip it, Louis."
"No, it's this. There's a party outside parked in a Caddy convertible. Party got here about a half hour ago. Party asked for you. I said you were out . . . went out, didn't come back yet. Party said would I point you out when you do get back? Worth a twenty to me if I pointed you out."
"So? Did you point?"
"I don't point out nobody till I ask. So I'm asking. If you tell me no, there goes the twenty, but I don't point. If you give me the okay, fine. That's the way I work, Mr. Chambers. I ain't been a doorman twenty-two years for nothing."
I grinned and I patted the back of his neck. "You just earned yourself an extra ten plus the twenty you're going to earn." I dug in for a ten dollar bill and donated it to Louis. "Point away, fella. Kind of, it'll be a late point. But tell the party I just came in and what my apartment number is. Only give me a little time to get up there first."
"Thanks. Leave it to Louis."
Upstairs, I put on the lights and opened the windows. Clean breeze of early morning freshened the apartment. I didn't think twice about my prospective visitor. That's the kind of business I'm in: clients drop from everywhere and their visiting hours have all the regularity of a berserk banshee. Within five minutes the buzzer rasped and I opened the door.
I didn't expect what I got.
I got pulchritude, all dressed up.
The lady was tall and cool with thick blond hair, braided and worn like a crown over her head. Her face was smooth and round, her nose thin and tiny, her eyes blue and clear—and impertinent. She wore a white mink stole over her shoulders, white gloves, and there was a gold mesh evening bag in her hand. She said, "May I come in?"
I stopped staring and rediscovered my voice. "Please do. Please come in."
She swept into the apartment and I followed her. She moved about for a few minutes inspecting pictures and doodads, said, "Nice," a few times, added, "You've a lovely place here."
"Thank you."
She removed the stole and placed it over the back of

an easy chair. She was wearing a black evening gown and little gold high-heeled shoes. Her arms were long and white and smooth with dimples near the elbows. Her shoulders were beautiful, wide and strong and without bones. She had a proud, statuesque figure and she was about twenty-eight years old, though with a lady like that you never can tell: she could be twenty-one, she could be forty.

"I'm a messenger," she said.

"Suits me. Suits me, whatever you are."

Now she smiled, a youngish smile, and one thin eyebrow moved up a trifle, quivering. "May I sit down?"

"You may do whatever your little heart desires."

"Very gallant." The mouth arched in a broader smile. She sat perfectly at ease, the gold bag in her hand, and she crossed her legs. The smile went away. She said, "I come as a messenger. I'm to ask a few questions and perhaps answer a few. May I?"

"Of course."

She sighed deep, blurted: "What's your interest in Eddie Adams, the late Mrs. Dorothy Adams, and the events surrounding an attempted burglary that took place a year ago?"

"Just like that?"

"Uh huh."

I went away from her. I paced the far end of the room, opened a cigarette case, brought it to her, but she shook it off. I lit one, returned the case to its table, said, "What's it to you?"

"It's nothing to me. I told you, I'm merely a messenger."

She shrugged her white shoulders. "You needn't talk to me if you don't want to. That's entirely up to you."

I paced some more. Then I stopped in front of her. "I'm a private detective."

"So I hear."

"By the way, name's Peter Chambers. What's yours?"

"Olga."

"Olga . . . what?"

"Just Olga, for the time being." Again a small shrug of the expressive shoulders. "Let's get back to the business at hand. Shall we, Mr. Chambers?"

"As I said, I'm a private detective. When business is lousy, you look to stir it up. I'd been going over some old newspaper clips and I came across that Mamaroneck deal. I figured it might be productive."

"Productive? Of what?"

"Money, naturally."

She was silent a moment, frowning in thought, her red

lower lip coming out in a pout. Then she said, "You have a client?"

"No client."

"You mean you're in on this on your own?"

"That's what I mean."

Now her blue eyes had more appraisal than an auctioneer hunting for a bargain. She looked me over, slowly, up and down, cocked her head, her nostrils opening slightly, and a queer smile hinged a corner of her mouth. "Very enterprising."

"Thank you."

"Very handsome, too."

"Thank you."

Silence again. Then she stood up, her dress rustling. She opened the gold bag and laid five one thousand dollar bills on the coffee table.

I said, "What's that?"

"That's to let sleeping dogs lie."

"Why? What happened up there? Why should anybody want to pay me to lay off? What's the pitch, lady?"

She came near me, near enough so that I could smell the light perfume she wore. "No pitch, Mr. Chambers."

"But—"

"As I told you, I'm a messenger. But a messenger with certain delegated powers."

"Power to pay me off? Why?"

"Because Mr. Edward Adams runs a shindig out in Jersey that's a very delicate proposition. Mr. Adams can't use publicity, adverse publicity, that is. That thing is running great guns out there. We want it to run as long as possible. A delicate proposition like that—it can go boom at any time. Bad publicity mushrooms up. Bluenoses move in. Anything can happen. We want to prevent that." She pointed to the money on the table. "Let's call that . . . part of the operating expenses."

I shook my head. "No good."

"More?"

"Maybe."

"It's blackmail."

"Is it? If there's nothing wrong on that Mamaroneck deal . . . where's the blackmail?"

"It's blackmail of another sort. Mr. Adams is running wide open in Jersey. His name starts poking up in the newspapers, crusades can start. Like that, I mean, it's blackmail. And I think you know it, Mr. Chambers. I think that's why you started prying. You're using that Mamaroneck business, perfectly proper as it may have been, as a lever."

"You're beginning to insult me, Miss . . . Olga."

"You insult beautifully." Again the queer little smile. "Would an additional five thousand salve the insult?"

I didn't answer.

She said, "I'll be frank with you. I've been authorized to go as high as ten thousand. That's take it or leave it. After that, you're on your own. If I were you, I'd take it. I wouldn't want . . . *to be on my own.* Mr. Adams is a kindly man."

"Is he?"

"But even a kindly man, driven into a corner, has violent reactions. What do you say, Mr. Chambers?"

"I'm leaving it."

She looked at me for a long moment, the inspection narrowing her eyes, then bent to the table, picked up the money, and put it back into her bag. She came back to me, moving slowly, came close, so close her body touched mine. She lifted her head, looking up at me, said softly, "Do you know me?"

"No."

"Ever see me before?"

"No."

"Ever in your life?"

"No."

The pressure of her body was more palpable. There was a throb in the soft voice. "Is there anything *special* you're looking for out of this deal?"

"Maybe."

"It's liable to work, brother. Funny as it sounds, it's liable to work." She raised up on her tiptoes, kissed a corner of my mouth lightly, turned quickly, retrieved the stole from the chair, slung it over one shoulder, crossed to the door and went out.

I shot the bolt after her.

Early morning sun tinctured my bedroom a pale yellow as I climbed under the covers. Sleep was quick and comfortable but I remember one last mutter: "Casey Moore, I love you."

I awoke at noon. Six hours' sleep isn't much, but sometimes it's enough. It was enough this time. I woke up refreshed. I showered, shaved and breakfasted. The phone kept ringing all the time but I didn't answer. There was a lot of stuff piled up in the office and my secretary was probably frantic but it would have to wait. I checked the Hotel Montero in the phone book, waited for a silence between ringings, grabbed at the phone and called Casey. I told him to stay put, that I'd be with him shortly.

I stuck my head out the window. It was a hot day, the sun boiling down. I dressed in slacks, loafers, a sport shirt and an odd jacket. The lights were still burning in the living room, almost invisible in the glare of the afternoon sun. I clicked them off and went out. There was a ticket on my car but even that didn't disturb me. I drove up to the Montero, obtained his room number from the clerk, and went up to Casey.

"Hi," he said.

"You too, fella."

"Any developments?"

"I think so." I recited the facts, omitting no detail. I said, "Casey, lad, I'm with you. All the way."

"Why?"

"Because, somehow, somewhere along the line, I think something stinks."

"How do you figure it, Mr. Chambers? True enough she offered you money, but her reasons sound plausible, don't you think?"

"Maybe. Maybe not."

"How do you make it, Mr. Chambers?"

"You may as well start calling me Pete."

"Okay."

"Like this I make it. What adverse publicity? Suppose I rake it up and there's nothing to rake . . . where does the publicity come in? Newspapers publish news, not nonsense. They wouldn't publish a rehash of a case that was closed last year, not unless new facts came to light. Dig me?"

"Yes. But perhaps, knowing they are skating on thin ice, they don't want *any* sort of *possible* adverse publicity. Happens, doesn't it?"

"Maybe. Maybe she was telling the truth—but if she wasn't, and that's much more likely, then it's a ruse, ten thousand dollars worth of ruse, to keep me off it. I'm going along with the second theory for the time being."

Musingly, he said, "Ten thousand dollars . . ."

"Don't make a martyr out of me, pal. I'm just not put together that way. I don't take that kind of money, never have, never will. But don't let me get on a philosophical pitch. It's either you've got larceny or you haven't. I haven't. I like to earn my dough."

He didn't say anything. He smoked his cigarettes.

I said, "You eat yet?"

"Yeah."

"Want to take a ride?"

"Where to?"

"I'd like to get a look at your father's house or what's left of it. I'd like to sort of mosey around the neighborhood. How's about it?"

"Fine with me."

Flushing, Queens, is rather remote for me. It took us about thirty minutes over the Queensboro Bridge, Casey directing me. The area around Whitehall Place was small, almost rural. The community was a square block of old houses, a tiny shopping center, and nothing else. Fanning out from Whitehall Place were unpaved roads losing themselves in shrubbery and flat empty lots.

I parked and Casey talked to me. He pointed out where 116 had been. It was levelled now, a square ragged expanse of nothing, black char of the fire still showing on the ground. Opposite was a small grocery store. A bent old man came out carrying a large shopping bag.

"That's Simon," Casey said. "He's been the delivery boy as far back as I can remember. I ought to go out and say hello."

"No you don't."

His head shot around toward me and his face was questioning.

"There's a lot of people around here," I said, "that you'd like to say hello to, I'm sure of that. You haven't yet, have you?"

"No. I've had other things on my mind, as you know. But I've been planning to drop around."

"Not yet, Casey. Not while our thing's cooking."

"But why?"

"Because, so far, there's only me. No client, remember? I don't want it spread around that you're back. If there's going to be a fall guy, let it be me. I know how to handle it. It's part of my business. Make sense?"

"But why should you stick *your* neck out? I've got a pretty good neck of my own."

"One neck is easier than two. Mine's already out. Let's keep it as uncomplicated as possible. Anybody's going to do any chopping, let them chop at me. Stay with me, pal. Okay?"

He smiled and shook his head. "You're the boss."

Simon was ambling back from his delivery. I got out of the car and hurried across. I called to him. "Simon."

"Yeah?"

"Talk to you a minute?"

"Sure." He came to me, a bent seamy-faced man, grinning

with yellow teeth. "What's botherin' you, young fella?"

I pointed at where 116 Whitehall Place had been. "I'm checking on the fire there."

"Aincha a little late, young fella?" His voice was a cackle, and the pleasant grin was as much a part of his face as his forehead.

"I'm from the insurance company. We're doing a recheck."

"Didn't know old Henry had insurance."

"Small policy. We've been holding the proceeds for his estate."

"Estate? Ain't no estate. Ain't no family left. One son. Heard he got killed, the poor kid. Off in that ol' Koree war. Mess, that Koree."

"They turn up sometimes even when they're reported dead."

"Yeah. Sometimes they do."

"What's your full name, Simon?"

"Gordon. Simon Gordon. You're makin' me feel right real important, young fella. Ain't nobody been asking old Simon any real fact questions for years and years now."

"Would you like to sit down somewhere?"

"Nope. I'm right comfortable standin'."

"Did you see the fire, Simon?"

"Nope. Happened around eleven o'clock at night. I hits the hay come nine, never later. Sleep like a top. Even them old fire engines don't wake me up. Sleep like a top. Nuthin' wakes me."

"I see. What about Henry Moore? When'd you see him last?"

"Know about ol' Henry?"

"I heard."

"Turned out to be a crook, ol' Henry. You wouldn't believe it. Got all hitched up that same night, ol' Henry did, upstate somewheres. Got all shot up, ol' Henry. You'd never believe it. Nobody talks about it around here, nobody says a word."

"When'd you see him last, Simon?"

"Saw him that selfsame day. Saw him that day, day of the fire, only the fire was at night. He was sittin' out on the steps of his house, a-whittlin' on a hunk o' wood, all dressed up, just sittin' and whittlin', till that car draws nigh and picks him up."

"What car, Simon?"

"Search me. It was close onta five o'clock. I'm just bringing a bundle over to the Wyatts, two houses down past Henry's, when the car pulls up, real fancy car too."

"You see who was driving?"

"Sure, I see. Man gets out, that's who was driving, and

he talks to Henry and Henry ups and off they go in the fancy car."

"Can you describe that man?"

"Nope. I ain't the least good in describing nobody, young fella. Couldn't even describe you to you, right now. But I don't forget a face, that I can tell you. I got what they call a . . . a photographic memory, that's what I got. I can give you back a face that come up against me thirty years ago, that I can. But don't ever ask me to describe 'em, because that I can't."

"The face of the man that came out of the car . . . would you remember it?"

His eyes became crafty. "You figure maybe he was an accomplice of ol' Henry up there upstate?"

"Maybe."

"I saw that bird, young fella, saw him good." He tapped a gnarled thumb against his chest. He was proud as he said: "You put me in front of a hundred people and have that guy be one of them, and I'll pick him out for you, sure as shootin'. But don't never ask me for no descriptions. What you call a photographic memory, a lot o' people got it, it's like a gift." He glanced about, tapped my shoulder. "Look, I gotta be gettin' back to the store. They'll be wonderin' about me. Sure hope I helped you, young fella."

"Thank you, Simon."

He looked at me with faded eyes, almost blankly as old men will, then he winked deeply, nodded, raised a hand in a half wave, and went off. I returned to Casey in the car.

Casey said, "Hot in here. Wow."

I started the motor and we shoved off. I said, "Queens is Long Island, isn't it?"

"Right."

"How long will it take us to get out to the shore? Cool breezes by the shore."

From a corner of my eye I could see him twist his head toward me. I could feel his eyes on me. But since I wasn't talking, he wasn't asking questions. "Yeah," he said. "Cool breezes by the shore. You make a right turn two blocks from here, then we hit the Parkway, then it's about a half hour."

When we arrived at Long Beach, there were cool breezes, and there was the tonic smell of salt in the air. Sun hammered down, coming back at us in a glare of white reflection. I said, "I wish we had time for a dip."

"Haven't we?"

"No. We're going to pay a visit. Lido. Maybe Mr. Adams is back from his yachting trip. Which way?"

"Turn left."

We stopped in the town of Lido and inquired at a drug store about the Adams estate. We were given directions which we followed to a large pink-roofed house near the sea. Tall, iron gates were open. We drove through, and up a pebbled roadway, and we stopped at a wide stairway leading up to two massive doors with brass adornments. I said, "Stay right here, Case."

"Here we go again. Why?"

"Same reason. I don't want people knowing you're around."

I got out and ran up the stairs and banged at a brass knocker. A butler opened the door and screwed up his mouth in a sour smile. I said, "I'd like to talk to Mr. Adams."

"He's not at home, sir."

"It's important."

"Please come in, sir."

It was like a cool tomb, the floor of glistening highly polished stone, the ceiling domed and far away, two stairways in the rear curling upward and, on each side, five heavy, carved oak doors. But there was no place to sit.

The butler said, "Just one moment, sir."

He went to one of the oak doors, opened it, and passed through. I waited, literally cooling my heels. Then the door opened again and another man emerged. He was thick-shouldered and squat and he approached me with more bounce than a hansom over cobblestones. His ears didn't match. One was pulpy. Aside from that, his face had the blue sheen of a tough-to-shave beard but it was pleasant. He was neatly dressed in a white linen suit, white shoes, and a dark blue sport shirt with no tie, collar over jacket. He was very polite. He smiled, said, "How do you do?" His voice was deep and raspy.

I said, "I'd like to talk to Mr. Adams."

"I know. The monkey told me. He said you said it was important. How?"

"Pardon?"

"How important?"

"Matt Bennett sent me."

The smile closed to lips squeezed together and his chin wrinkled. He pondered a moment, then: "Would you wish to talk to the Missus?"

"I would, if Mr. Adams isn't at home."

"He ain't."

"Didn't know he had a wife. I thought she—"

"He has. Kindly follow along."

He wheeled and I walked behind him. We went to the rear between the two curling stairways. He slid apart glass-brick doors opening on a long wide corridor at the end of which was another set of glass-brick doors, bright light of sun filtering through. We traversed the corridor and he pushed open the second set of doors and we were on a broad, railed terrace fronting on landscaped gardens. Off to the left, some distance, was a swimming pool, surrounded by wrought-iron chairs and tables and long comfortable padded beach chairs. One of the beach chairs was occupied. It was candy-striped and it contained a lady. The lady wore a black bathing suit and large-lensed sun glasses. The lady had blonde hair braided over her head like a crown and her name was Olga. The bathing suit paid off on the promise of the evening gown. She was high-breasted, narrow-bellied and full-hipped, and the figure, curve upon curve down to long-legged smoothness, could bring the blood to a froth in your brain. If you were a man. If you were a woman, you might sniff.

She was using a pen on a writing tablet in her lap. As we approached, she glanced up, and turned on a small smile for me, prim and almost involuntary like a college professor looking up from an enforced reading of the funnies. My guide said, "Guy wishes to see Mr. Adams. Wishes also to see you. Says it is important. Says Matt Bennett sent him."

"Thank you, Mike."

She moved the glasses down on her nose, looked at him upward and dismissed him with the wave of a finger. Mike bowed a clumsy bow, turned, went back up the terrace and into the house. Olga laid the pen and tablet on a nearby table, reached for a frosted drink, sipped and set that back on the table. She was not wearing gloves now; gloves, with her costume, would have been most inappropriate. The diamond marriage ring on her finger was very obvious. She said, "Something special, Mr. Chambers?"

"I wanted to talk with Mr. Adams."

More sharply she said, "Why are you here, Mr. Chambers?"

"I told you. I hoped I'd find Mr. Adams."

"You think you might make a better deal with him?"

"Possibly."

Her tongue came out and licked wetly at her lips. I couldn't see her eyes behind the glasses but she cured that. She took them off and laid them aside. She kept her left hand upraised, the ring glinting in the sunlight. Languidly she said, "Surprised to find that I . . . am Mrs. Adams?"

"Yes."

Her smile was no longer prim. "Simple and to the point, aren't you? You could be nice if you tried."

"I have been trying . . . Olga."

"Don't try too hard, Mr. Chambers." Her voice was a lilting tease. "I'm a newlywed."

"How long, Mrs. Adams?"

"Four months."

"And already Eddie Adams is out on his yacht . . . with close friends . . . but without you?"

It didn't work. The smile stayed on her face. She said, "Mr. Adams is past sixty. I'm twenty-four. Mr. Adams is entitled to his recreations and his rehabilitations without me."

"Smart," I said.

"Mr. Adams wouldn't have married me if I weren't smart. Mr. Adams has a great contempt for fools."

"You're no fool."

"Aren't I . . . ?"

She threw up a look that wasn't the look of a newlywed.

I shifted my ground. I said, "When's he due back?"

"Don't know. My husband is, to say the least, unpredictable. There's a letter from him." She pointed at the table. "It's all right. You can read it. No billing and cooing. Not Mr. Adams."

I lifted the letter. There was no envelope and no date mark. It was short and to the point. It said the fishing was good and the weather was good and he was relaxing. He hoped that she was enjoying the short vacation from him and that he expected to be home soon.

"When," I said, "is soon?"

"With Eddie Adams you don't know."

Suddenly there were hands on my shoulders and I was whirled around. I shoved the letter in my pocket and I was ready to swing when other hands caught mine and pinned them behind me. Mike, smiling in front of me, said: "Paul tells me there is a monkey with one arm sitting outside on your running board taking the sun."

I said, "Who the hell is Paul?"

"Me," said a voice behind me and grip on my hands tightened.

Mike said, "Who's the monkey?"

"My assistant."

"And who the hell are you what needs assistants? I thought you said Matt Bennett sent you?"

Olga's grin was pure joy. Olga was having a good time.

Again the tongue came out, licking the lips. "All right," she said. "Let him alone."

My hands were freed and the man behind me came into view. He was young, tall, dark and beefy with nasty eyes and thick red powerful hands.

I said, "You jump a guy from behind like that, Paul, you're asking for trouble."

"I like trouble, mister."

Olga said, "Okay, boys, break it up."

Mike was insistent. "But he said Bennett sent him."

"Bennett didn't send him. It was his way of getting in here."

"Oh, a wise guy," Mike said.

"Maybe too wise for his own good." She extended her hand for her glasses, set them on her nose, tilted her head upward but I could no longer see her eyes. "I'm being kind to you, Mr. Chambers. Maybe my reasons are as special as yours. But, for the time being, suppose we say . . . au revoir. You don't mind if the gentlemen show you out."

"Good-bye, Mrs. Adams."

"Bye, beautiful."

I could hear her laughing as they marched me up the terrace and through the corridor and into the tomb-like stone lobby, and they held the door open for me and slammed it behind me.

Casey stood up from the running board, grinning. "Saw a couple of real hood types around the premises. I was beginning to wonder whether you needed me. They give you a hard time?"

"Nothing important."

"Get any dope?"

"Adams is still at sea."

We drove back and stopped at the same drug store that had given us directions. It was ten minutes to five. I said, "I want to make a call in New York. Wanna come?"

"Personally, I've got a yen for an ice cream soda."

"Good idea. So've I."

Casey was lustily sipping through a straw while I made my call. Information gave me the phone number of the Coronet Life Insurance Company, Number 10 Wall Street, and the operator put me through after I inserted hollow-sounding coins. I asked the switchboard girl for Herb Wiley, and I got him. "Hello?" he said.

"Herb? Pete Chambers."

"Hi, Pete."

"Herb, how about dinner tonight?"

"Okay, if you can make it late. Eight-thirty, or so."

"Eight-thirty is fine. How about Casa O'Brien?"

"Perfect."

"And Herb . . ."

"Yes."

"Dig up a file for me. And bring it with you."

"File?"

"Beneficiary, Edward Adams. Deceased, wife, Dorothy Adams.

"We cover that?"

"Yeath. Date of death, May 11th, last year."

"Hold it a minute, Pete." I waited, fingering the wall of the phone booth, and then his voice came back. "Okay. What's up?"

"Tell you when I see you."

"Casa O'Brien. Eighty-thirty."

"Swell."

The Casa O'Brien was a delightful restaurant on East 64th Street. It was owned by a man named Abramowitz. It was quiet, dimly lit, sound-proofed, the spacious tables far removed from one another, and the walls covered from floor to ceiling by the murals of Ichabod Rally, one of our brilliant young American geniuses. Rally never painted a canvas: he worked only on walls. Rumor had it that Abramowitz had not paid Rally, but that they had arranged a contract whereby food and drink would be afforded to Rally for the rest of his life or the life of the restaurant. There were those who said that Abramowitz had effected the best bargain of his life but I doubted it. I knew Rally and though I didn't know his capacity for food, I did know his capacity for potables. Anyway, the Casa O'Brien, owned by a man named Abramowitz, featured exquisite Chinese food and, on a small balcony, an Austrian zither player named Hapsburg who zithered the Third Man Theme almost exclusively. But he zithered it softly.

I was alone at a corner table, sipping a stinger and waiting for Herb Wiley. I had showered and shaved again and I was dressed in one of my dark blue suits. Some of the sun from the shore had hung on to me and I was, somehow, rested and relaxed. I was just about ordering the second stinger when Herb showed up.

Herb Wiley was one of the vice-presidents of Coronet. Herb had been a football player at Harvard and he had served in the Army with me. Herb had some distinguished streaks of grey in his hair now and he was slightly gone to fat, but he carried a lot of weight down at Coronet and he was a bright, alert executive who earned his keep.

We did small talk all through the meal but when the liqueur showed up, I said: "Where's the file?"

Herb said, "I don't need a file."

"You know the case?"

"Know it thoroughly. I reviewed the file."

"What do you think of it, Herb?"

"Cut and dried."

I smiled and shook my head. "The police say: open and shut. This guy says: cut and dried. Seems I haven't got a chance."

"Chance?"

"To upset it."

"I wish you had. They'd run me a testimonial with speeches, if I could haul back two hundred thousand out of left field."

"That ten percent deal still go?"

"It's a standing rule, Pete. Any investigator that can show us where a fraud was pulled—ten percent of the money recovered is his fee."

"Brother, you just hired yourself a man."

"Glad to have you. But if you're talking about the Adams case . . . there just isn't a loophole. Matter of fact, our own investigators only reveiwed it about a month ago. Routine. We do one check-up about a year later."

"How's Adams fixed right now?"

He grinned with square teeth. "You mean could we recover our two hundred thousand?"

"I mean something like that."

"You show me fraud and we pay you at once, that's how good Adams is."

"Really?"

"He owns that club out in Jersey, owns it outright; he owns a showplace out at Lido, owns it outright; he's got a yacht; he's got property here in the city; and he's got a load of stock. And he made practically all of it during this past year. Quite a man, Eddie Adams."

I sipped on a sticky after-dinner drink. I said, "What about the gun, Herb, that killed Dorothy Adams? Supposed to have belonged to this Henry Moore."

"Belonged all right. Registered in his name and the bullets that killed her came from the gun. Paraffin tests showed that he fired it. Mrs. Adams, before she died, told her story clearly, and identified Henry Moore to the police, or should I say the corpse of Henry Moore. There's just no out there, Pete. None whatever."

"And Matt Bennett was a witness?"

"No witness was needed, really. Mrs. Adams' story would

have been enough. Bennett was merely corroboration as was Adams himself. Certainly, Adams was guilty of no crime. He shot a burglar in his own home, a man who had already critically wounded Mrs. Adams."

"What about the open door downstairs?"

"Can happen, can't it? People leave doors open."

"But it was Adams himself who left that door open."

"So what? The attempted burglary occurred at two o'clock in the morning. Adams came home at one. He may have been overtired. As a matter of fact, it's the police theory that he may have been a little tight though they can't prove that."

"Anybody fix his whereabouts for that evening?"

"Of course. At about that period his Diamond Circle was going out of business."

"Failed completely, didn't it?"

"That's right. Suddenly lost its lure for the customers. Happens. Real live joint, that circle. Knew a show-gal there once, a nymph by name Olga Owstrowski. Wow, and wow-ee?"

"Blonde?"

"Yeah. Were you there too?"

"No, but the name, Olga . . ."

"Shaped out of heaven, was Olga."

"What do you mean by nymph?"

Herb tried to look wicked, which was about as successful as painting circles under the eyes of a cherub. "Guess," he said.

"Know what became of her?"

"Don't know a thing. Never knew *anything* about her, really, except her hobby."

"And what was that?"

"Men. What else?"

"Okay. Let's get back to the Diamond Circle."

"Well, Adams poured a lot of money into it, trying to recoup. But he finally gave up."

"What's that got to do with his whereabouts of that evening?"

"He had an office right above the club."

"So?"

"He was there, practically all of that evening, right up until midnight, working on his books."

"Any corroboration of that?"

"None necessary. There was no reason for any suspicion. Furthermore, it couldn't possibly be disproved."

"Why not? Figures to be an elevator man, something, maybe a secretary he was working with."

"Uh uh. The office was one flight up, a walkup, separate entrance from the club. Adams had a key to the outside door, downstairs; and to the office door proper, upstairs. And he worked alone that evening, no secretary. I'm wondering, Pete, whether you're not pushing where nothing can fall. If ever a case was cut and dried, this is it."

"Yeah, maybe, maybe so."

The waiter came with the check and I grabbed it. Outside, I said, "Can I drop you somewhere, Herb?"

"You can drop me at home." His forehead creased. "You driving? I thought you didn't drive in town."

"I'm going across to Jersey."

"Jersey?"

"A little unfinished business."

Unfinished business got me to the Stardust Room at ten-thirty. I left my car in the roadway with the lights on. And I left my hat in the car so I had nothing to check. I walked through the dimness to the stairway, and up the stairway into the bar. It was seething with more customers than the lobby of the Garden on fight night. I moved to the carpeted stairs and ran down. I knocked on the door of the office of The Manager. It was opened by Frankie Gold. I shoved in and hit him quick. I caught him flush on the chin and he fell, face forward like he'd been hit with an elephant gun.

The door had a barrel bolt and I shot it.

I'm an old hand at my business. I worked fast and silently. I removed his tuxedo jacket, his tie, his suspenders, the gun from his holster and a silk handkerchief from his jacket pocket. I used the tie to knot his wrists together behind him. I used the suspenders to bind his ankles. The handkerchief became a silken gag across his mouth. I lifted him, laid him out behind a long leather couch and tossed his jacket over him. Then I picked up the gun, crossed to the polished black door, and reached for the knob—but it had no knob. It was the type of door with one knob and that one on the inside. Smart man, Matt Bennett. I used my own handkerchief now. I put it across my mouth, held it with my left hand and rapped on the door with my gun muzzle.

Matt Bennett called: "Yeah?"

My voice came from deep in my throat, choked against the pad of the handkerchief. "Open up, boss. It's Frankie."

"What's the matter?"

"I got somethin' stuck in my t'roat. Open up."

The door opened and I jammed the gun in his stomach. You could feel it going in. Good living had softened up

Matt Bennett and you go soft first in the belly. "What . . .?" he said. "What . . . ?"

"Where's Frankie?"

"Sleeping. I borrowed his gun."

"Sleeping?" Then it hit him. His face lost a little color and he backed away. "What do you want?"

"Nothing." I kicked the door shut with my foot.

"You didn't keep your promise, Matt." I put my handkerchief away.

"What promise?"

"About my being here. About out little chat."

"How do you know?"

"Never mind how I know. You didn't did you?"

He kept his mouth closed.

I waved the gun. I said, "You're going to talk, Matt."

His eyes moved with the gun. "You wouldn't dare."

I sighed. I said, "Matt, you know me pretty good. I'd dare. And I wouldn't be taking any chances. It's Frankie's gun. I plug you, wipe it off, stick it in his mitt, shoot another bullet out of it and blow. Nobody knows I'm here. Now it's Frankie's party and let him try and talk his way out of it. You wouldn't be able to help him. Because you'd be slightly dead."

Matt Bennett was nothing if he wasn't a reasonable man. The bit of color left in his face disappeared entirely. He said, "What do you want?"

"Where's Eddie Adams?"

"On his yacht."

"Did you tell him?"

"Yes."

"How?"

"He's got one of those gimcracks. Ship-to-shore phone."

"What'd you tell him?"

"Told him you were here. Told him what you told me and what I told you. That's it, Pete. I work for the guy. I wouldn't hold out information on him. But what's the excitement? I don't get it."

"Doesn't he trust you, Matt?"

"Sure he trusts me."

"Then why'd he send Olga?"

"Send Olga for what?"

"To negotiate with me. Eddie must have used that ship-to-shore phone again. She offered me ten thousand dollars to lay off. I'm asking you—why?"

There was sweat on his face now. Earnestly, he said, "I don't know why, Pete. I swear to you."

"She told me the publicity wouldn't do this joint any good. You think that's a reason? You're an ex-lawyer."

"You know how we operate here. It's like living on the side of a volcano."

"Very poetic. But just because I'm nosing into an old deal—how does it come up publicity? Figure that one for me."

He shrugged. "You might blow it up to something. Why the hell are you asking me? I didn't make the offer, did I?"

"Look, pal. What happened up there in Mamaroneck?"

"Nothing that the cops haven't got. I gave it to you straight, Pete. I swear."

I looked at him, looked at the gun, looked back to him. "Matt, I play hard, and you know it. I want to know what happened up there. It'll be confidential, I promise you."

"You've got it straight, I tell you."

"Maybe I have, but if I haven't, you're it, Matt. You. If you're handing me stuff on the bias, I wouldn't want to be you. I wouldn't want to be you for nothing. Last call, Matt."

His eyes were wild, and there was fear in them but he said, "You've got it straight, Pete. You know what I know. Believe me."

I believed him.

I said, "How long has he been married to Olga?"

"Four months."

"That the chick used to be at the Circle?"

"Yeah."

"Owstrowski, that the one?"

"Yeah."

"You ever sleep with that, Matt?"

His complexion was better, and his eyes had stopped rolling. "No. Loves it like candy, that one. But she picks her people."

"Never picked you, did she?"

"No. Maybe I don't have sex appeal. She thinks there ain't a guy in the world wouldn't want to have her. Maybe she's right. So . . . she donates her favors . . . where she pleases."

"Did all right with Eddie, didn't she?"

"Smart chick, no question."

"You got a gun, Matt?"

"What? What's that?"

"You got a gun? Here?"

"Yeah, sure."

"Don't use it."
"I don't intend to."
"I mean now. I'm leaving. If you're not mixed up in anything, don't start mixing now. Check?"
"Check."
"Go back to your desk and sit down. If you want to make a ship-to-shore phone call, make it. You're on your own now. I'm leaving, and I don't want you to start buzzing any of your hard boys outside. Check again?"
He went to his desk chair and fell into it. His smile was an automatic exposure of teeth. "Good-bye, Mr. Chambers. And don't worry about my hard boys."
"I'm not worrying."
I went out and let the door slam behind me. I wondered for a moment how they got in without a knob, decided it must work on an electric apparatus with a button on the outside, moved to Frankie Gold stiffly, slumbering behind the leather couch, dropped his gun beside him, and went out and up the carpeted stairs.
The throng at the bar had not diminished. I pushed through, squeezing against people, said, "Pardon me," pushed some more, and then a warm hand spread over my hand and tugged gently and I turned to face Olga Adams, née Owstrowski, smiling sweetly. She wore a red dress that began deep beneath her shoulders and ended in a wide swirl on the floor. She said, "Busy little boy, aren't you?"
"Always trying to earn a buck."
"Can I buy you a drink?"
"No thanks."
"You just beg for trouble, don't you?"
"Do I?"
"I saw you come in. I figured you'd be going out with marks on your face."
I took my hand out of hers and touched my cheek. "How's it look?"
"Good as ever. Let's sit, eh? Let's sit and chat a couple of minutes, eh?"
"I'd rather not."
"Then let's just chat, eh?"
"Not here."
"Where?"
"Outside. In my car. With the motor running."
"Real careful, aren't you?" Her blue eyes looked up to mine, and fluttered. "But can *I* trust *you?*"
"Let's find out, Mrs. Adams."
"You twisted my arm."

Outside she waited on the marble steps, while I got the car. Wind whipped in the Jersey air like the spring breeze had come to a boil. The sky was thick with clouds of rain and thunder talked in the distance. I drew up by the stairs and opened the door of the car. She ran down and got in beside me. I leaned over, touching her, pulled the door shut, rolled a short distance, stopped, braked, kept the motor running. I fixed the rear view so that I could see who was coming out of the Stardust. I said, "All right, let's chat, Mrs. Adams."

She kept her distance, huddled in the opposite corner, but her voice was soft. "You can call me Olga."

"What's it all about, Olga?"

"I saw you come in."

"I could have called down to Matt."

"So?"

"I didn't."

"Why?"

"Why . . . ?" She seemed to be thinking. I grabbed a quick glance at her. There was a little frown between her eyes and she was rubbing a finger at her nose. For a moment, behind all the careful makeup, I could see the little girl. For a moment, in the dimness, it was the round face of a spoiled little girl, a cute little girl, a little girl running to school, blonde hair flying, a little girl who had not grown up yet to curves that had the boys panting around her, tongues hanging out. For a moment I had an inexplicable affection for her. Then my eyes went back to the rear view. She said, "It's a good question." She was silent another minute. Then she said, "I don't know. I wish I did know. If I'd called down they'd have been waiting for you. Anything could have happened."

"You against violence?"

"No. That's got nothing to do with it." She was closer to me now. I could feel the heat of her thigh. "I don't know. You're a guy trying to hustle a buck. I suppose that can't be held against you. A little bit, you're beginning to aggravate me. A little bit. Not all the way. Not yet." Her voice dropped. It was almost a whisper. "I think maybe you can earn your buck, maybe you can earn your dirty blackmail, and maybe you can get away with it. I've been thinking. I've got a small hunch it's not just money you're after."

"No?"

"No. That's my hunch, and it's a pleasant hunch." Her hand rubbed at my knee. "Tell me the truth, did you know about me?"

"I don't understand."

"Did you know I was Eddie Adams' wife? That part of your play?"

I let it go. I didn't answer.

She said, "Did you know I danced at the Circle?"

"I know now."

"Danced." She chuckled. "I walked around, practically naked. You've got to have a certain special qualification to walk around practically naked, and do nothing else."

"Must be," I said.

"Okay, that's my hunch. You want to pick up some dough and you also want to work your points. Maybe you're going to come out all right, all around. Anyway, that's why I didn't call down to Matt."

I did two prim nods and a blink. "And me thinking you don't believe in violence . . ."

"Not yet, I don't. The hand on my knee moved upward. "You'll know about it when I come around to that. I'll let you know. I rattle before I strike. I rattle good and loud."

"You rattling now?"

"Now I'm purring which may be worse."

"You build yourself up pretty good, little girl. Do any dramatics when you went to school?"

"How do you know I went to school?"

"I can tell by the way you talk."

"Would have loved to be an actress. Spent all my time in the movies . . . my town didn't have legitimate plays. Wound up on the stage, all right, walking around naked with feathers."

"Yeah," I said.

"Real talkative, aren't you?" The hand was as high as I could take it. "I'll tell you this, mister. You figure to catch up with a lot of grief and there's nothing I'm going to be able to do about it. That's the men's department. And I'm not the men's department. I think you're stupid but cute."

"What happened up there in Mamaroneck?"

The hand went away, abruptly. She moved back to her corner. "You know what happened in Mamaroneck. You know, just as I know—from the newspapers. But you're trying to roll it up to something big, aren't you?"

The rear view gave me Frankie Gold. Frankie Gold was coming down the marble steps, peering into the gloom. I said, "That's all, sister." I opened the door on her side. "Good-bye, Mrs. Adams."

"Bye, stupid."

The minute she was out, I braked off, shoved into gear

and rolled. Thunder was sharp and there was lightning to the east. On the road fat drops blotched the windshield. By the time I got to town, I was fighting a storm. New York, I love it, but the climate is the worst in the world.

When you can't sleep, you can't sleep, and fighting it does not help. I listened to disc jockeys during the night and to chamber music and symphonies and jazz. I listened to rain in the streets and looked out on the bleary yellow lights of the misty city. I thought about Olga Adams and her smooth shoulders and her soft inquiring hand and her blue eyes and the look in her blue eyes. I thought about her promise to rattle before she struck and I believed that promise. Olga Adams had an ego all her own and Olga Adams didn't think I was using blackmail solely as a prod for money. No. Olga Adams thought my motives were more devious. Let her think. As long as Olga Adams thought along those lines I was safe—from Olga Adams—from violence directed by Olga Adams. But in the meantime, there was Matt Bennett and Frankie Gold and the remote Eddie Adams.

I pushed thinking out of my mind. I concentrated on blackness. I counted slowly. I counted fast. I didn't count at all. I tried self-hypnosis. But sleep would not come. I climbed out of bed and brought back magazines and thick books and paper-backs, and I read until at long last it was morning, and I was engulfed in the euphoria of false energy that frequently happens after a sleepless night.

I bathed and shaved and ate and dressed and wrapped a raincoat around me and went out into the terror of morning. In my business I can sleep late and usually do, and morning and the creatures of morning are strange to me. My car was parked tight to the curb near the house but I whistled down a cab.

My secretary's eyes popped at my matutinal invasion of the office but I pretended not to notice. Routine had piled up and we went to work on it. Rain plopped sadly all morning and all through the early afternoon. At two o'clock fatigue mixed with boredom and I quit. I left the raincoat in the office and had lunch in a nearby beanery. When I came out the rain had turned to fog and the steam was coming off the streets. I went back into the beanery and phoned the office and said I wasn't coming back. It was a brown and dirty day and I was ready for sleep. I took a cab home, paid, and the cab rolled off as I stood under the canopy of my apartment house and breathed deep of the thick air. Central Park South was deserted. Anybody with any brains was indoors. A car started up from the curb, picking up speed, and—before I dropped—I saw the black prong extending out the window. Bullets from a carbine splattered above me and the car roared off.

I got up and dusted wetness from my clothes.

I had a hunch that Eddie Adams was home.

I parked the car outside the Montero and I used the house phone to call up to Casey Moore in the event he had company. Casey Moore didn't have company. A creaky elevator took me up, and when Casey opened the door for me, I said, "Shove over, pal, I'm moving in."

"Love to have you but I don't think I've got the room."

"Got to be room somewhere. It's a hotel, no?"

"Something like it. Why you moving in?"

"Because I can't go home. Remember I told you to keep your neck in?"

"Yeah?"

"That was a general precaution. Now it's special."

"What happened?"

"Bullets. A profusion of bullets out of a rolling car with yours truly as the target. They figure they get rid of me—they get rid of trouble. They don't know I have a client."

We went downstairs together and Casey's friend, Joe Vincent, took a room, payment in advance since he had no baggage. Up in Joe Vincent's room, I got out of my clothes and stretched out in bed and Casey lit my cigarette and he lit his own. I blew smoke toward the ceiling. I said, "Help me, Casey."

"Me? I wish I could."

"Think, boy. Is there something? Anything?"

He didn't think. He said, "There's nothing. I was away. For a long time. Remember?"

"Any relatives, Case? Your father have brothers and sisters? Your mother?"

"Nothing. It was that kind of a family. My mother was an orphan. She was an only child. My father has an older brother in Ireland, but I wouldn't know how to get in touch with him if I wanted to."

"What about friends? Didn't your father have friends?"

He hesitated a moment. Then he said, "I suppose he did, but they were just people, casual, nobody close, nobody he'd really confide in . . ." His voice trailed off. He looked uncomfortable.

I sat up in bed. "You holding out on me, kid?"

"Yes." His eyes avoided mine.

"But why?"

He prowled the room, then he picked up an ashtray and

sat down at the foot of the bed. "It's something I . . . I thought I shouldn't talk about. It's one of those things you know about but you don't talk about because . . . because, well . . . you feel that people wouldn't understand."

"You may as well tell me, Case."

"I suppose I should, though I don't see how it can have any bearing. Which is why I didn't mention it. Which is why I'm reluctant right now."

"Let's try, Casey."

"It's a lady. Her name is Mary Davis. I used to call her Auntie. I always think of her like that—Auntie. Dad and she were friends, real friends, for eighteen years."

"They ever think of getting married?"

"She . . . had a husband."

"I see."

"No you don't. That's the point. That's why it's so hard to talk about. Auntie—Mary Davis—had a husband, Fred, Fred Davis, who was an invalid, paralyzed. He had suffered a spine injury on his job as a milkman. He had slipped on ice one winter many years ago." His eyes closed and suddenly, for the first time, his face had the look of a boy. "As far back as I can remember old Fred sat in a wheel chair, motionless, and he couldn't talk." Now his eyes opened. "They had a tiny little income, some sort of compensation from the milk company, and the two of them lived like that in a tiny spotless little apartment in the Bronx."

"How'd your father meet her?"

"Years ago, he was a bank guard in a Bronx branch. He met her up there before he was transferred downtown. She had a little thrift account. She was the sweetest, finest person I've ever known."

I bent over, used his ashtray and got rid of my cigarette. I said, "What's so tough about talking about that? I don't get it."

"For eighteen years my father and this lady were close, intimate friends. But friends, Pete, nothing more. People don't understand that sort of thing. People read into these relationships, people love to gossip . . . and there was gossip about my father and Auntie, there was gossip indeed."

"Sure," I said.

Casey smiled but it had no happiness. "Dad was a lonely man and Auntie was a lonely lady. They saw a great deal of each other. As a child, I used to spend week-ends up there, with my father. As I grew up and broke away, Dad would spend week-ends up there himself. But there was nothing wrong, please believe me. Fred Davis loved it.

He couldn't talk, but there was a manner of communication —he could sort of talk to them with his eyes. It was a fine, good, decent relationship."

I said, "I begin to understand your reluctance to talk about this."

"These things are so frequently miserably misunderstood."

"Your father would have married her, I suppose, had it been possible."

"No question about that. But she was married and to a man Dad loved. When I grew up, Dad and I talked about it, often. All he was ever worried about was gossip hurting this angel of a woman and her sick husband. As a matter of fact, as the years passed, they built up a little fib among them—for the neighbors, for people in general—Dad and Auntie were supposed to be brother and sister, and my calling her Auntie became real. Can you understand this?"

"Of course I can."

"As time passed, it was almost as though they believed it themselves; in time, practically, they became brother and sister. Auntie was tiny, wispy, sweet and timid; and Dad was big and bulky and hearty; sort of the big brother, helping whenever he could, carrying Fred around; bringing presents like a television set; you know, things like that. They got old together, Auntie and Dad and the invalid, Fred."

I folded the pillow and lay back on the bed. "I assume you've seen her since you're back."

"She's the only one I tried to see. But she's gone. She doesn't live there any more."

"Gone? Where to?"

"Miami, Florida. So I was told by the people who took over the apartment."

"How long?"

"About six months."

"Did you get the address?"

"Nobody had it. The only information I was able to get was that she had moved down to Miami, to a sister, a married sister."

"Did they know the sister's name?"

"No."

"Do you know anything about this sister?"

"I'd heard about her. She'd lived in the city of Miami most of her life, and had married there."

"And you don't know her name?"

"Only a first name, Alice."

"What about Auntie's maiden name? Do you know that?"

He thought a moment. "Maxwell. That's it. Maxwell.

Mary Maxwell." He stood up and laid the ashtray on a table and dumped his cigarette.

I said, "Do you have a gun, Casey?"

"Luger," he said. "Souvenir."

"Is it in working order?"

"It is."

"Bullets?"

"Plenty."

"Get it in shape, pal." I looked at my wrist watch. "I'm going to catch some shut-eye. Wake me about seven."

"Why the questions about the gun?"

"We may have to use it. I've got two, one at home and one at the office, but Pete-Chambers-Joe-Vincent isn't showing up at home or at the office, not until this gets a little cleared up. I think another visit to Lido is in order."

"When?"

"This evening. And you're coming along as bodyguard."

"It's about time I got into some action."

"I hope there won't be any action, but who knows?" I yawned, jaw-creakingly. "G'bye, Case. Go play with your Luger." He was at the door when I called to him: "What was the name of the milk company old Fred worked for?"

"Certified Special. Here in Manhattan."

"G'night."

He closed the door behind him softly. I got up, turned the key in the lock, looked out the window on the fog beginning to blow away, pulled the blind, stumbled to bed and went to sleep.

Shrill sounded the phone. Shrill as a shrew and ceaseless as a shrew on the right side of an argument. I rolled over in bed and reached out a hand and picked up the receiver and said, "Go away."

"Pete? It's me, Casey."

I woke up. "What time is it?"

"Seven. Banging on your door didn't help. I'm calling from my room. I told the girl to keep ringing till you woke up."

"Stay with it, kid. I'll pick you up in fifteen minutes."

I hung up and used the phone again for Information. I got Edward Adams' number in Lido, called and the connection was made. I asked for Eddie Adams and a voice said, "Who's calling?" and I said "Peter Chambers," and the voice said, "Hold the wire," and then there was a pause and then there was another voice, slow and cool: "Yes? This is Mr. Adams."

"Pete Chambers."

"Yes, Mr. Chambers?"
"All right if I drop in on you, sir? This evening?"
"I'll be here."
"Swell. And Mr. Adams . . ."
"Yes?"
"There are people who know I'm coming out to see you."
"I beg your pardon?"
"This afternoon I almost got in the way of the well-known hail of bullets."
"I don't understand."
"Just mentioning it. Just mentioning that if it happens again on my way to see you, or coming from your place, well . . . there might be people who'll get the wrong view . . . especially since they know I'm contemplating a visit to you."
"Now look, Mr. Chambers . . ."
"Let's skip it, Mr. Adams. I'll see you within the next couple of hours."
The trip took us one hour and fifteen minutes. Casey Moore was silent most of the way. He had no holster and the thick Luger was a bulge in his jacket pocket. Once he said, "Do you make it for trouble?"
"I doubt that."
"But this very afternoon—"
"That was this afternoon. This Eddie Adams is a smart operator. He won't pull anything where he can be tied into it. I may be wrong, of course. Which is why I've got you around with that thing in your pocket."
That was the extent of the conversation until I braked in the roadway outside the pink-roofed house. I said, "Keep the thing in your lap and don't hesitate to use it—if necessary."
"No. They'll know you're out here. What they won't know is whether I've got others staked out around the premises, and like that we've got them off-balance which is good."
I patted his chin with the back of my hand, got out, ran up the stairs and worked out on the brass knocker. This time the door was opened by Paul and Mike was right beside him.
"How do you do?" Mike rasped. "You wish to see Mr. Adams?"
"I wish."
"You do not object, I hope, to a gentle frisk by Paul?"
"I do not object."
Mike smiled at Paul and Paul passed expert fingers over my person. "Clean," Paul said.

"Smart fella. And now, if you will come along this way . . ."

He led me to one of the oak doors, opened it, nodded, and swept his hand in front of his stomach in a shoveling grotesque gesture bidding me enter. I went in and he closed the door behind me.

It was a large room with plum-colored walls and a coral carpet and heavy, carved, shining mahogany furniture. Soft light dripped from a high-up chandelier with many bulbs. Two broad windows were festooned with heavy drapes, alternately striped in plum and grey. Set between the windows was a massive mahogany desk. Behind the desk was a chair like a throne, turned-around-back-to-me, the tall carved rounded rear cushioned in brocade. The room was silent, the thick walls and the heavy draperies shutting off all outside sound. I flicked an impatient glance about me, waiting.

I thought I was alone.

I was wrong. I had never been more wrong in my life.

Noiselessly, the high-backed desk chair swung around and Olga Adams rose out of it. Olga Adams, completely nude. Correction. Olga Adams, completely nude, except for high-heeled gold sandals, painted toenails protruding. She came toward me slowly, undulantly, her hair unbraided in a gold cascade flowing down her shoulders. It was enough to put a cramp in your gut. I looked away fast, saw the thrown, creamy-white housecoat on a chair in a far corner and a wide gold mesh belt over that. Then I looked back at her, at all of her: Olga Adams coming toward me.

"Eddie Adams," I blurted. "I called him."

"I know."

"I want to talk to him."

"Talk to me first."

"But he knows I'm here."

"Not yet he doesn't."

"But Mike, and that other hood . . ."

"They're devoted to me."

Then she arrived, and hung her hands around my neck.

I hunched back stiffly. I said, "Eddie Adams . . ."

"He's upstairs. He doesn't know you're here yet. And he won't—until I want him to."

She pulled up on me and her lips opened on mine and she kissed me, softly at first, a kiss like a caress, then harder, the sweet-smelling body clinging, one knee moving; and then it eased off, and it stopped, and her hands dropped from around my neck, and her blue eyes were narrow and questioning and stony and unbelieving, and her mouth was tight. She looked at me for a long moment, narrow-nosed with fury, her expression almost childlike. Then she flung away, turned, moved away from me, and I watched her go. She lifted the housecoat, slipped into it, zipped it up, placed the gold belt around her waist and fastened it. Then she came back to me, a throb in her temple trembling.

"So that's not it," she said.

"No, Mrs. Adams. That's not it."

"What, then, *is* it?"

"Easy, lady."

"Look, you. It's not money. Ten G's would have been beautiful for a guy on a small hist. I've been around, fella. Ten G's, and you'd have been out clean. But you didn't want it—so it's more than dough. I'm good at things like that. I'm a chiseler myself, a high-class chiseler. I thought . . ." Her eyes travelled over me. "Okay, I was wrong."

"You're right about that."

"What?"

"That you were wrong."

She backed away and regarded me. She hooked her thumbs in the gold belt. "All right. If it's not dough—what is it?"

"I've got an answer, lady. But it's not gentlemen-like."

"Let's hear."

"Mind your business."

The thumbs came out of the belt. "I'm minding my business, fella. That's exactly what I'm doing. What do you take me for?"

"I don't know, Mrs. Adams. I'm not taking you for anything. I came here to speak with your husband."

"You'll speak with him, right now, right after I've finished my say. I saved you from a beating, maybe worse, at the Stardust. When you came here the first time the boys were going to work you over, but I talked them out of that. Reason—I thought you had ideas. You say I was wrong. Okay, maybe *I* had ideas. Well, I don't have them any more."

"Fine. Now I can talk with Mr. Adams?"

"Sure, but first hear me. I'm declaring myself in. I promised I'd rattle. I'm rattling, right now."

"But why?"

"Figure it for yourself. I married a guy named Eddie Adams. Tell you a real big secret—I'm not in love with him. Guess why I married him."

"I can't imagine."

"I'm a chiseler but, like I said, a high-class chiseler. Eddie Adams is rich, and he's going to be richer, and he's not going to live forever. I don't know what you're up to but whatever it is, in the long run if it hurts Eddie, it's going to hurt me. So . . . I'm declaring myself in. Actively. Eddie likes others to do things for him. Not me. I like to do things for myself. That's all, brother. Lecture finished. I've rattled."

"What about your theme song?"

"What theme song?"

"Publicity. You get jammed up, it's as bad as Eddie getting jammed up. Like that nobody gets richer."

"Leave it to me. You'll get caught up with, brother, and caught up with bad—and there won't be any publicity, there'll be nothing, except you, maybe, dead."

"Now can I speak with Mr. Adams?"

"But of course." She went to the door, opened it, smiled sweetly, waved, went out and closed the door behind her. I puffed out my cheeks and blew breath in a long wheeze. I wiped my face with a handkerchief, wiped my lips, and looked at the handkerchief. There was no more than a faint smudge of lipstick on it. Then the door opened and closed softly and a man came toward me, a tall, slender, graceful man, his silver hair neatly combed.

"Mr.Chambers?"

"Mr. Adams?"

"I'm Eddie Adams."

"How do you do?"

I put the handkerchief away and we shook hands.

He said, "May I offer a drink? Brandy?"

"Scotch, if you will. One cube. And water."

"Certainly."

He had a soft mellow voice. His face was smooth and pink from the sun. He had a pointed, high, finely-boned nose. He had a cleft in his chin and he had thin lips. His eyebrows were dark and smooth and long, his eyes narrow, of a greenish color with brown-gold flecks. He carried himself high, moving gracefully, as though there were a good deal of power in his slender legs. He wore a charcoal grey perfectly-fitting suit, narrow black pointed shoes, a white shirt with a flowing collar, and a grey tie with small maroon figures. He went to a liquor cabinet in a corner, opened it to glistening bottles and glasses, and prepared my drink, using silver ice prongs on a silver ice bucket. He poured brandy for himself in a small snifter glass. He came back and handed me my drink. His hands were delicate, with thin blue veins and long fingers tapering to highly polished nails.

I said, "Thank you."

"Not at all." He lifted his glass and smiled without meaning: his face creased and his lips pursed, the skin lifting around his cheekbones and crinkling his eyes. "Good luck."

I sipped and set my drink down on a round, long-legged table with a leather top. He looked me over carefully and then his eyes rested on my forehead. He said, "I'm an old man, Mr. Chambers."

When you get that, it requires no reply. I brought out cigarettes, made my offer, was shaken off. I lit up and blew smoke.

He said, "I'm sixty-three. My time for excitement is over." He sipped, looking at me. I tried to catch his eyes but I missed. He aimed his about a quarter of an inch over mine. It's a trick and a disconcerting one. He said, "I leave excitement to younger men, men like you." Suddenly the eyes dropped, and grabbed at mine and held them. "What do you want here, Mr. Chambers?"

"Talk," I said. "Chatter. But face to face."

He went away from me to an easy chair. He sank into it and crossed his legs. "What have we to talk about, sir?"

"Mamaroneck. Henry Moore."

"And what, precisely, face to face, is there to discuss? About Mamaroneck? *Or* about Henry Moore?"

I couldn't say : *Mr. Adams, you've got me there.* I couldn't say: *Tell you the truth, Mr. Adams, honest I don't know.* This was Eddie Adams, whom I'd never met, but whom I'd heard about, a wise old bird who knew every bluff in the book. I'd met him now and I wasn't going to go shooting-fish-in-a-rain-barrel. Not with Eddie Adams. So I resorted to the oldest device in my trade: I looked wise, said nothing, and smiled dourly. And waited.

Eddie Adams said, "I'm a business man. I came up the hard way. Waiter; bartender; maître d'; owner of a small club; owner of a fabulous operation—The Diamond Circle, that suddenly went sour; and now the owner of another highly successful venture, the Stardust Room. I've been through the mill. I've been down and up, and down and up again. There's no more time—for struggle."

"By struggle, sir—do you mean me?"

"I mean you're a young man, punching to get ahead. More power to you. But I'm a business man, remember. I admire a good business man. And I abhor a fumbler."

"Fumbler? Again—do you mean me?"

"You've been offered ten thousand dollars—only because, in my old age, I just don't choose to fight. You turned down a good price, young man. If you press further, you get nothing, because in that case, it would be good business on my part, to resist, to fight. The only possible reason you're here now is to attempt to increase the figure. I say you're wasting your time."

I played with that. I said, "If it's worth ten thousand, why isn't it worth more?"

"Because, in actuality, it's worth nothing. What I mean is this. You've dug around and come up with a bit of worthless tripe. But—this very tripe may, under certain circumstances, be exaggerated by, let us say, enemies of mine. Suddenly, a going business is in jeopardy. At my age, I don't want to fight it. So I offer a price just to get it out of the way. But I won't be made a sucker of."

"I repeat, sir. If it's worth ten, why isn't it worth more?"

"Because I'm a business man. Because I know value, even nuisance value. And supposed you agreed to the figure, and I paid you. The question would always remain as to whether or not you wouldn't start it up again at another time."

"Isn't that always the risk in paying . . . ?"

"Blackmail?" His forehead furrowed and his eyes squinted.

"So it's called, I hear."

"There are two answers to that question. One is violence. When this kind of dirty money is paid, the payee, assuming he has any intelligence, realizes it's a one-shot deal. You press a sucker . . . you're asking for trouble, panicky trouble, and that's the worst kind. Somehow, psychologically, that works."

"What's the other answer, Mr. Adams?"

"I don't propose to stay at the Stardust too long. Perhaps another year. I'm husbanding my money for a change. One more year, and I can get out of it, get out of all of it. As I said, I'm getting on. I've had it, all of it. I want to take it easy the rest of the way, I want to coast but I want to live right."

"I see."

"I'm attempting to be absolutely honest with you. Perhaps . . . at the close of the year . . . I'd be willing to pay again." He wriggled a finger at me. "Just to keep you honest."

"How much?"

"An additional ten thousand. After that, I wouldn't care. I'd be out of it."

"Pretty good for one visit."

"I beg your pardon?"

"One visit, face to face, and I've doubled the ante. Despite all the prattling about good business."

He stood up and he came near me. His voice was very soft. "We can set up a legal contract, for services rendered, something like that. The lawyers can work it out. Ten thousand now. Ten thousand a year from now. That's it, Mr. Chambers. That's it, in all finality. How's it sound?"

"Stinks."

Blood went out of his lips and his jaw muscles lumped.

"Get out of here, please. Quickly. Please get out of here."

"Let's not lose our heads, Mr. Adams."

A slender hand reached out and seized my lapel. His breath came in spurts. "You've got more to lose than I have, Mr. Chambers. You've got a long life ahead of you. I have just a little time left. I can afford to be careless but you can't. Think about that, sir." His hand opened on my lapel and fell to his side. "Remember, it's easy for me. I'm too old for struggle. I can always"—he shrugged, expressively—"go away, go out of life. I've had it and I'm a little tired. But not you. You're young and vital and the future is long and rosy for you."

"Any more?"

"That's all. Think about it Mr. Chambers. It's an uneven contest, and I stand all to the good. Think and if you change your mind, call me And now . . ."

He walked to the door and opened it.

Mike was grinning in the doorway.

Eddie Adams said, "Mr. Chambers is leaving."

"Yes, sir. Kindly follow along with me . . ."

New York provides everything for everyone, including an all-night haberdashery where I was able to purchase underwear, shirts, socks and ties. A drug store furnished shaving equipment. I loaded my bundles into the car, drove to the Montero, deposited Casey and his Luger, went to Joe Vincent's room, and picked up my sleep where I had left it at seven o'clock.

Sunshine woke me early. The weather was fair again and warm. I attended to my ablutions in a strange bathroom with temperamental faucets and at nine o'clock I was in a tailor shop having my suit pressed while I smoked cigarettes in a cubicle. At ten o'clock I was in the offices of a milk company, Certified Special, and I was being directed to the Head of Compensation who turned out to be a large man with the flutters and a pink tie. His name appeared on a bronze name plate on his desk. Seems foolish, a man alone in an office with a bronze name plate on his desk. In this instance it was not foolish: Certified Special had a certified special reason for a name plate on the desk of Head of Compensation. It stated in raised letters: Mr. BLATHINGSQUYTZE. Mr. Blathingsquytze, I learned very quickly, was more stuffed with self-importance than a wrong-choice pompous traffic policeman magnified by his first and brand-new badge.

I said, "I should like to inquire about a Fred Davis whom you have on your compensation lists for a good many years."

"Yes?"

"I'm a private investigator."

"Yes?"

"Mr. Davis used to live in the Bronx. About six months ago, he removed to Miami, Florida. I'm in the employ of a firm of attorneys."

"Yes?"

"Mr. Davis has come into a small inheritance. I've been retained to skip-trace his new address."

"Yes?"

"I'm certain that such new address has been put through to you people. For the purpose of forwarding his checks."

"Yes?"

"Would it be possible for you to inform me of this new address?"

"Sorry, confidential."

"But this is to Mr. Davis's benefit."

"Sorry, confidential."

"But, look, Mr. uh . . . uh . . . this is a small matter. Nothing more than a change of address."

"Sorry, confidential."

"I'm working on a job, Mr. B. You can help me out. What's the difficulty?"

"Any information of this nature," he said, his voice moving up to a thin soprano, "may be procured by the presentation to me of a Court Order, duly signed by a Justice of a Court of Record, or by a copy of such order, duly certified as such by the Clerk of the Court. Do I make myself clear?"

"Now look, pal . . ." I sighed and dug out my wallet and reached in for the traditional twenty and waved it like a flag of truce.

Mr. Blathingsquytze looked as though he were going to faint. "Sorry," he squeaked. "Confidential." And then, his voice soft as a breeze in the trees, he added: "Oh, my . . ."

I stood up, glared at his name plate, glared at his pink tie, turned on my heel and departed Certified Special.

I walked to the subway and took the train to Wall Street. Number 10 was imposing, and the offices of the Coronet Insurance Company covered all of the 11th floor with a receptionist facing the elevators. Receptionist. They must have plucked her out of the front line of the best musical in town, and given her a tight blue blouse to strain against, and there was plenty to strain. Her smile added gleam to the sunny morning. I said, "Mr. Wiley."

"Assuredly. Would you care to give your name?"

"Assuredly. My name is Peter Chambers."

"Thank you. Won't you sit down?"

I didn't sit down. Standing, the view was better. She wrote out a slip, and pressed a button. Swinging doors opened and another musical comedy number appeared. The receptionist handed her the slip, smiled at her, smiled at me and then bent to answer a phone that tickled a tiny tinkle. The messenger didn't strain in front. She strained in the rear. She wore a roomy white silk blouse and a very tight blue skirt that divided her into fetching half moons, and as I watched her go back through the swinging doors, I thought how nice it would be to spend all of one's working day in the quiet confines of the 11th floor of Number 10 Wall Street. I was anticipating the return of the young lady in the tight skirt, but I'm sure Herb Wiley stymied that on purpose. The phone tinkled again, the receptionist answered, and this time she hung out a brand-new smile for me. She pointed. She said: "Through those doors, Mr. Chambers. Third room to the left."

Third room to the left was a frost-glass door which swung open on Herb Wiley surrounded by wood-paneled walls. He came up from his desk and we shook hands. He said, "How goes it with Adams?"

"Nothing yet. I'd like to get straightened away on a couple of items. That file still clear in your mind?"

"No." He grinned. "That's the kind of mind I have. Just a minute." He lifted the phone, talked into it and dropped it. He said, "Make yourself comfortable, sleuth." He plumped into his swivel chair, swiveled, and looked out the window.

Door-knock, and Herb called, "Come in."

The young lady in the tight skirt brought a file and laid it on his desk. We both watched her going out. I said, "No boy messengers at Coronet?"

Herb was pithy. "Girls are prettier." He opened the file. "What's your problem, Mr. Chambers?"

"Bennett was a witness. Right? Who else?"

"Adams, himself."

"Okay for those two. Now what about the servants? That's been rankling in the back of my head. House up there. Should be servants."

"Should be and there were." He brought a sheet out of the file, read it, said, "There was a butler and his wife. But they occupied a small house about five hundred yards to the rear. They came out after a while but they weren't actual witnesses. The thing was over and done with by then. What's the next item?"

"Jack Rawlings?"

"Who dat?"

"Look in your lovely file."

He looked. He said, "Adams' partner. We've got data right up to the re-check. What do you want to know?"

"He isn't Adams' partner any more, is he?"

"No." He tapped his finger on a typewritten sheet. "They chipped in on the venture, took them about six months to build it. It was a lot of money but I don't have the exact figure. Adams bought him out practically as soon as they went into active business."

"Why?"

"I don't know."

"You got a file. They have a falling out?"

"I don't know. My investigators didn't get this information directly from Mr. Rawlings. Mr. Rawlings doesn't live here any more. Furthermore, this data is no more than padding, has no relevancy to the case."

"Any idea where Rawlings lives?"

"Lemme look." He shifted his papers, talked without looking up. "He's got a daughter."

"Hooray for him."

"Name of Jane."

"Real romantic."

"Lives at 666 Park Avenue. Only child."

"Where does *he* live?"

He found it. He looked up. "Lives at the Hotel Empress."

"Where's that?"

"Miami Beach."

"Miami Beach?"

"What's so shocking about that?"

"Nothing. May I use your phone?"

"Sure."

I called the Montero and the girl gave me Casey Moore and I said, "You ought to have a drag with the airlines."

Casey said, "You want to borrow a plane?"

"Not that drastic. I want passage for two to Miami."

"Two? Who's going?"

"You and me. Think you can arrange reservations?"

"I'll try. Just between you and me, if you want fast action—it's easier to borrow a plane."

"Let's do it the hard way. De Luxe, and don't lay out any dough. First available flight. Bye. I'll see you at the hotel." I hung up.

Herb said, "All the way to Miami with a friend just

to talk with Mr. Rawlings. You sound like one of *my* investigators. *With* an expense account."

"Expense account?" I looked at him, hopefully.

He shook his head. "You're what is known in the law as an independent contractor. You're working on your own. You might earn a fee and you might not. But your expenses are your own. And that de luxe round trip you were just talking about, that should go you about a hundred and sixty dollars. Each."

"Any cash around here?"

"Of course. This is an insurance company. How much?"

I had a conference with my wallet. I said, "I've got two hundred and thirty. How about five hundred?"

"You ought to be good for that."

"Ought I?" I extracted a wrinkled mad-money blank check and made it out for five hundred to cash and presented it to Herb.

Herb said, "Come with me."

I trailed him through many corridors to a cashier's cage where he okayed my check and I obtained my cash. Somebody buttonholed him and he said, "All right, Pete. Keep me informed, eh?"

I said, "How do I find my way out of here?"

His grin was the grin of an imp. "You're a detective."

"No no-pants guide for Peter?"

"Peter'll manage."

Herb Wiley and his macabre sense of humor.

Casey wasn't home but there was a message for me in Joe Vincent's box. Casey had written: "Big spring traffic. Tough as all blazes. I'm going down to attend to it personally."

Upstairs, I kicked off my shoes, hit the bed and dozed, and by the time Casey returned, it was late afternoon. He knocked and I called, "Who?" and he said, "Casey," and I roused up and opened the door. He grinned and he said, "How's tomorrow morning?"

"Fine. What time?"

"We leave La Guardia at ten."

"Ten," I said. "Wow. I'm a reformed guy. I'm an early morning prowler."

Casey said, "I'm hungry. How about chow?"

"What else we got to do?"

We ate and we walked across to the park, and we loafed and we chatted and I learned more about his father, and about his early life, and about Auntie, and then we strolled back and picked up the evening papers, and it was seven-thirty in Joe Vincent's room when I went to shave.

"What's with shaving?" Casey said. "Going somewhere?"
"Nowhere. Force of habit."
"You've got to be up early tomorrow."
"Wanna make a movie with me or something?"
"Nope. I'm going to hit the sack early."

I shaved and bathed and dressed to the teeth; navy blue suit, sparkling white shirt, shiny black shoes, navy socks and a righteous deep maroon tie. Casey said, "Where to?"

"Honest, I haven't the faintest notion."

He grinned. "You look right handsome, man."

"Then I know where I'm going."

"Where?"

"To interview a lady. If she's home."

"Lady?"

"I hope."

The elevator took me down and I walked out into the night. I had time to kill and there was no reason why I couldn't kill it and try to pick up information at the same time. Rawlings was in Miami, but the daughter was here, and so was I with nothing to do. What could I lose? Nothing.

I went to the car, plucked off another ticket, moved it to another parking spot, waved at a cab, and said "666 Park Avenue" which turned out to be a tall, slender, red brick building with a triangular-type canopy and a doorman with enough braid to warrent a salute. I saluted, and he grinned and saluted in return and I entered a plush lobby, soft-lit with amber lights, and in the charge of another uniformed gentleman without a hat but with a starched dickey.

I said, "Jane Rawlings?"

He smiled and said, "7 A."

A silent elevator took me up to 7 and I wandered about the geometric angles of a meticulously clean modern corridor until I discovered A. I dabbed at the button of 7 A, and a voice called, "Come in," and I twisted the knob and pushed into a lavish apartment.

I was in a square foyer. Three steps down was an expansive living room, French doors opening upon a terrace, skyline of New York framed like a picture in the background. A thick coral carpet ran wall to wall, all the way from the door by which I had entered to the wide French doors at the far end. There was enough furniture to fill a warehouse, but it all fitted into the hugh room, neat and comfortable and modern (but not too modern), the wood a deep-grained blond, the decor a blend of coral, black, grey and gold, in perfect taste, perfectly balanced.

I saw the lady in profile. And there was enough of the lady to see. She wore a shimmering rose-red cocktail gown and she had one foot up on a high hassock, adjusting the strap of a rose-red shoe, and incidentally, affording me a view of as shapely a limb as ever it had been my pleasure to observe. I observed but she didn't even look toward me. Impatiently, she said, "Come in, come in."

I went down the three carpeted steps and I stood there like a mummy waiting to be wrapped. The lady completed Operation Shoe, lifted her dress and adjusted a garter belt (as though I were a lady caller . . . and maybe she thought I was . . . she hadn't even glanced my way). Then she straightened up and turned toward me.

You could have knocked me over without a feather.

You could have blown at me and I would have toppled.

I knew the lady. Everybody knew the lady. If you were a student of the rotogravure sections of the Sunday papers (and how many of us are who are students of nothing else)—then you had seen her riding a horse to hounds, or climbing an Alp, or watching them do the cancan in the gayest spot in Paris, or looking at a ruin by moonlight in Rome. If you by-passed the rotogravures—then you had seen her in motion pictures. She had perpetrated three sensational movies before she had become bored with histrionics, and had retreated from the menacing contracts dripping gold.

Jane Rawlings. The biggest thing in pictures. Literally.

I simply had not associated the name.

She was the tallest, fullest, truly shapely lady I had ever seen. There was about five feet, eleven inches of her, perfectly proportioned, and most of it a delicious throng within the shimmering rose-red gown, but not all of it. The dress was of satin, strapless and simple, descending in entrancing curves. Her arms and shoulders were smooth warm-glowing cocoa-olive. Her hair was long and black and thick and curly, swept across the back of her head and bulk-massed and smoothly glinting over one shoulder, a little ear exposed, burdened by a heavy dangling earring. Her eyes were black and enormous in an oval-shaped silk-smooth face, the high point of which was a pouting bold-curved mouth, shining deep red. She said, "Where's the tuxedo?"

"Tuxedo?"

"People just don't do thing right any more, do they?"

Blankly I said, "Don't they?"

"Seems they do not." Her eyes whisked over me in quick inspection. "At least you're tall."

"Six foot two, sometimes three, depends how I stand."

"That meant to be funny?"

"Am I supposed to be funny, too?"

"You're only supposed to be good-looking and that, I am pleased to observe, you are."

I was getting worried. How small can small talk get, how uninhibited, and how crazy? Maybe our lady had ridden one horse-to-hounds too many or maybe she'd climbed one extra Alp. I did my most pompous cough, twice, straightened up tall and in my severest tone I said, "Miss Rawlings, I came to talk to you about your father."

"You . . . *what?*" She actually looked frightened.

"Talk. About your father."

Now *she* did a double-take, slowly and her eyes puckered. She said, "Are you drunk?"

"No. Are you?"

"Now, really . . ." She went to a corner of the room where there was a black patent leather bar with five tall black patent leather stools. She twitched a finger at me. "Come here. You say you're *not* drunk. Maybe you ought to have a drink." I approached and she pointed behind the bar. "Anything you wish. And there's a refrigerated compartment for ice." Her eyes slid over me and there was an amused cast to her mouth. "Maybe you'd better pour one for me too. Scotch and soda, good stiff."

I tended bar and brought her a drink. I said, "Skoal," and we sipped. The door buzzer sounded and she said, "Get that, will you?"

I set down my glass and went up the three steps and opened the door to a tall dark young man wearing a tuxedo and a black Homburg. He didn't click his heels but if he had, it would have been appropriate. The whole look of him—it was something like an unclicked heel. With a flourish, he wisked off the Homburg, exposing sleek, black polished hair, and, enunciating carefully, and looking directly at me, he said, "Miss Jane Rawlings?"

I can get into the spirit of things. Profoundly, I said, "No."

Miss Rawlings came up behind me. The young man glanced a glance at me that was meant to be withering, looked over my shoulder, smiled with all the teeth, said, "Ah, Miss Rawlings. I am from Mr. Landon."

Laughter came behind me. Laughter gushed, deep and howling. I turned to find her almost doubled up, slapping at her thigh, laughing until her eyes brimmed over. She waved a hand weakly. "Go away. Away, lad."

"The lady," I said to the unclicked heel, "means you."

"But Miss Rawlings . . ."

"The lady says go away."

"Away," he said blankly, "says the lady?"

"Away . . . away . . ." she said between paroxyms.

"Away we go," I said and I hustled him out and closed the door on his expression of complete bewilderment.

I let her laugh.

I left her in the foyer roaring, and I went back into the living room, and I gathered up my drink, and I sat down on a soft chair and I waited, and I didn't have long to wait. She came to me, composing herself. She said, "Somewhere along the line, somebody owes someone an apology."

Non sequitur was in order. "I think you're very," I said, "lovely."

"Who are you?"

"My name is Peter Chambers."

"Chambers?"

"I'm a private detective."

"Detective? What are you doing here?"

"I came to—"

"I know, I know. To talk about my father." She got her drink, raised it high in the air, bowed, said, "Mr. Chambers, I believe I owe you an apology and an explanation. But upon one point I remain adamant. I think you're absolutely beautiful." Her eyes ran down my legs and her murmur was an amused purr. "And so tall, too. Tall, sitting, that's really tall."

"Miss Rawlings . . ."

"Ever hear of Ted Landon?"

"No."

"You wouldn't. It's an escort service."

"Escort service? I thought those things were outlawed. Licenses revoked, or something."

"True. But when anything, even a service, is arbitrarily revoked . . . and there is a genuine need for same . . . bootleg operations spring up."

I poohed. I poohed the best pooh I could manage vis-a-vis so beautiful a lady. "Bootleg escort service. Sister, how crazy can you get?"

"Brother, tonight *you're* my escort or I commit murder."

"Me?"

"I just dismissed my swain for the evening. Or didn't you hear?"

"I heard. And I offer myself as substitute swain."

"Good. But you've got to get into your tuxedo."

"That," I said, "is home."

"Then go home."

"I can't go home."

"Look, let's not go into crazy dialogue again. Let me explain this thing first, eh?"

"I'm all ears, Miss Rawlings. And eyes."

"Perfect," she said. "I'm going to love this evening." She moved into a chair near me. "You know me, I take it."

"I've been a lifelong admirer."

She made a long face and blinked her eyes. "Well, lifelong admirer, late this afternoon, I got a phone call from a press agent friend that I'm invited to a nighttime cocktail party at Toots' upstairs room given in honor of our newest screwball-type bombshell, Marilyn Mullaney. Marilyn is an old friend of mine. I knew her when she was sprawling background for calendar ads, and I'm dying to go to this party. Except."

"Except what?" I said, docile as a straight-man.

"Except, who's going to take me? This is a problem, dear sir, a thoroughly female problem, of which too many men simply are not cognizant. Who will take me?"

"Rough guess, I'd say—utterly conservative—about fifteen million able-bodied males throught these United States would gasp as the opportunity."

She wrinkled the pertest of noses. "Thank you. But remember, I'm a large one and my man must be over six feet tall. Tie that to the fact that, at the moment, I'm fresh out of boy friends. I mean people who interest me. And remember again, that the phone call came in only a few hours ago."

"I'm remembering all of it."

"That's where Ted Landon's bootleg escort service comes into wonderful usage, and you'd be surprised at how many of the best ladies of our fair city thank their high and low heavens for good old Ted."

"Me too, I think, in an oblique sort of way."

"You make your phone call to Ted, you state your exact specifications, and you are provided with an innocuous but perfectly proper escort that fills the vacuum beside you. The dictates of our culture are appeased. You have the arm of a man. You do not attend a party alone. Also, you are footloose and fancy-free."

"And *you* mistook *me* for one of Ted Landon's boys?"

"And a fine compliment you were to Mr. Landon's selectivity." Her smile dissolved to a serene expression of mock severity. "Now look, you're not going to let me down. I'd planned dinner and then the party."

"Sold. With one proviso."

"What's that?"

"That you don't regard me as one of Landon's innocuous

young men. No footloose and fancy-free. Very possessive type, me."

"You think I'm crazy. Very candid type, me. I think you're a godsend, and I'm going to cling to you until you holler. Now what's the deal about not being able to go home? You married?"

"No."

"Skip the rest of it. If you can't go home, you can't go home." She stood up. "You'll do without a tuxedo. What are we waiting for?"

"Now, about your father . . ."

"Uh uh. No business. For now, fun. Let's save that. Let's you and I get acquainted. Not a word of business. Let's get out of here."

We had dinner at the Big Club with violins. We went to Mullaney's party and I wasn't the only man without a tuxedo. I fell in love with Jane Rawlings but I fall in love easily, though as concerns Jane Rawlings, I challenge you not to fall in love, no matter how invulnerable you are. We quit Toots' upstairs room at two o'clock in the morning but I didn't take her home directly. I asked the cabman to drive along Central Park South, slowly. He did, and there across from the entrance to my apartment house two swarthy gentlemen paced the asphalt, avidly nonchalant. A cruise around the corner disclosed two more gentlemen at the back entrance, these more furtive, hallways operators as it were.

Eddie Adams had his boys out looking.

For me.

"Okay," I said, "Now we go home."

The cab let us out at 666 Park Avenue and outside the door at 7 A, Jane said: "You've been a darling. Come in now, and we can talk about business . . . whatever you like . . ."

"Thanks. But I think we can skip it."

"But—"

"It's late and I've got a plane to make early tomorrow. For Miami. That's what I mean about skipping it."

"I don't understand."

"Well, I can talk to the boss direct, can't I, down there. Miami. That's where your dad lives, doesn't he?"

She shoved the key into the door, roughly. She opened the door and when she turned, I saw she was crying. I said, "What the hell? Did I say something out of the way?"

"No."

"What's the matter?"

"My fault. I thought you knew."

"What?"
"My father. He's dead."
Silence. Silence for a long and miserable minute. Then I said, "Look, honey . . ."
"No. I want to go in now. Thank you for a lovely, lovely evening. You've been wonderful. And please call me when you get back."
And that was that.
Four hours in the heavens and you're in Paradise. Miami Beach in the springtime is Paradise on the best day Paradise ever had. There was a dry sweet breeze and swaying trees and a blue-green ocean and sumptuous hotels rising up to unflecked azure. We checked in at the Empress and though spring is the off-season and the rates are down, the down rates were stiffer than the posture of an embarrassed Englishman. We took a double room, payment in advance, and upstairs, four hours out of New York and at two o'clock in the afternoon, we looked out on tropical foliage and a brillant cobalt sky and the bright plumage of the deep South. We looked out also on a spacious swimming pool and the prancing adornments of the browned people. I said, "I've got to grab off a little of that sun. How about a swim?"
Casey's swift glance went to his empty sleeve and returned to me. "No swimming for Casey. I just haven't got used to being a one-armed guy. Not yet."
"Sorry."
"Don't be sorry. And if you've been trying to be a diplomat, let me tell you you've been highly successful."
"I haven't been trying, Case. What the—"
"Forget it. You go have a swim. I'll shower, and stick around here."
I called downstairs about swim trunks. I wanted someone to buy me a pair of blue boxer trunks, thirty waist, and I was told the boy would have them up shortly. When the boy arrived, I was sprawled nude on the bed and Casey was taking his shower. The boy was about sixty-five years old with a brown-red face and white hair and the strangest white eyelashes which gave him the look of a secretive father owl. I paid for the trunks and tipped him and asked him how long he'd been working at the Empress?
"Fifteen years," he said.
I pulled into the trunks and looked myself over in the mirror. I said, "Ever hear of a guy around here by the name of Jack Rawlings?"
"Sure. Used to live here."
"Dead?" I said.
"Yeah. Keeled over about three months ago. Heart attack.

He weren't a young guy, you know. Had a lot of dough and—"

"Thanks, pal."

"Don't mention it."

I went swimming in a tiled pool with cool green water tapped fresh from the ocean. I lay out and soaked up Florida sun. Then back in the room, I shaved, showered, slipped into shorts and a pair of socks, and went to work on the phone book. Casey was sleeping. I found what I was looking for: David Powers Protective Agency, Inc. Dave Powers, New York detective and old friend, had retired on a pension, moved to Miami and opened a small private agency. I called and I got through to him and we did chatter for a few moments and I told him I was *not* on vacation in Miami and finally it got around to: "What can I do for you, Pete?"

"I'm trying to locate an Alice Maxwell."

"Here at the Beach?"

"No. Miami proper."

"Married or single?"

"That's where it's rough, Dave. Alice Maxwell was her maiden name. I don't know her married name. But my information is that she *was* married in Miami."

"Beach, or City?"

"City, I've been told."

"Okay, Pete. Figures for a check of the records and a follow-through. It's too late now. When do you need your information?"

"Sooner the better."

"Okay, I'll go to work on it first thing in the morning."

"How much, Dave?"

"Twenty-five bucks, I imagine. No more, unless it breaks up somewhere unusual." He checkled. "You don't think I'd cheat you, do you?"

"Now that you're a private cop, who knows? Okay. 1502 at the Empress. Soon as possible."

"I'll get through to you in the morning."

"Swell. Bye, Dave."

I hung up and swung out on the other bed. Change of climate does something to the circulation, slows you down, something, makes you hunger for a nap. I could hear myself snoring before I fell asleep.

Casey woke me. He was all dressed. He said, "I'm all empty inside. Let's eat."

"Brother, you talked me into it."

We had dinner, late, in a swank restaurant and then we did the town. Casey found a girl, and then I did the rest of the town myself. When I rolled in at three A.M., Casey wasn't back yet, but when the banging started on the door and I woke up to see that it was eleven o'clock in the morning, Casey was spread-eagled on the bed wearing a beatific smile, but wearing nothing else except one shoe and one sock, both tidily in place.

I went to the door, opened it, said, "Sh. You'll wake my pal."

Dave Powers threw him a look and grinned. "Nobody'll wake your pal, pal."

I flung a sheet over Casey, and removed the shoe and sock. Casey's smile grew wider and he turned over and hugged the pillow. I fixed the sheet over him. Dave Powers said, "I'd like to have the dreams he's having. I'm afraid I'm too old. Who is he?"

"Client. Nice kid. You get my information?"

"Yeah." Dave was a short round man with bow legs and laughing eyes. "Her name is Alice Trenton. Husband is a mining engineer."

"Well fixed?"

"The worst. Husband is the wandering type and a heavy drinker. Never home. Job in Peru, job in Paraguay, job in Arabia. You know the kind. Sends money home when he thinks of it."

"Any kids?"

"Two sons. Both married. One's in Seattle, the other lives in Paris. Same deal. Send money to Mom when the impulse moves them. She's got a sister living with her now, sister and a sick husband."

"Pretty good for a fast check."

"Oh, I don't know. It's a small town, really. Once you get a line on people, and ask your questions in the right places . . . it's not New York, you know."

I shelled out twenty-five bucks. I said, "What's the address?"

"90 Blossom Street, City of Miami. Not the best neighborhood in the world."

"Thanks. Dave." We shook hands and he left.

I woke Casey which wasn't easy. His smile disappeared as sleep went away. "Large head," Casey announced.

"Get under the shower, and keep it on cold. We're going visiting."

"Whom?"

"Auntie."

"You found her? How? You've been with me practically since we arrived here."

"The ways of the private detective are most mysterious.

Or so we like the public to think. And you're the public. Go take your shower."

I ordered breakfast sent up with coffee, extra black. I hauled Casey out of the bathroom and we had our breakfast. He ate like a horse. I said, "How's the head?"

Casey said, "What head?"

I said, "The young recover quickly."

Casey said, "About Auntie. How'd you find her? I'm dying to know."

I told him and he looked disappointed.

I said, "What's with the face? Everybody wants glamour from a detective. You tell them about routine and all the shine gets rubbed off. Okay. Next time I'll work in Mata Hari, international complications, alphabet-bombs, and blood on the poop deck."

"Sorry," Casey said. "When do we go see Auntie?"

"Now."

There should be coins that have but one side. Snow should be on mountain tops and should never be mingled with the garbage of a city. A beautiful woman should not have an ugly voice. The transparent green of the ocean should remain unmarred by the sticky slick of oil. There should be dreams for the poets and the immature, inviolate dreams. A landscape should fix its point of glory and hold still forever. Paradise should remain unsullied, even around the edges.

And a resort town should not have slums.

A taxi took us across to the City of Miami, and tooled its way slowly towards heat and dilapidated houses and slovenly children, and hot rising odors, and limp wash exposed to the sun on sagging lines. 90 Blossom Street was a weather-faded, sun-blistered, slatted wooden bungalow with a lopsided shingled roof. It was hot in the cab and it was hotter when we emerged. Barefoot boys in bathing trunks were playing stickball in the street.

"I'd better go in alone, first." Casey said. "Remember she thinks I'm dead."

"Sure."

Casey walked up two warped wooden steps and knocked on the door. It was opened by a frowning woman in a print dress. Her hair hung loose and damp about her face and she had one hand up, pushing it back out of her eyes. This was not Auntie. I couldn't hear what they were saying but there was no expression of recognition on her face. Casey talked to her and then they went in and the door closed behind them. I watched the boys on the street playing stickball.

Ten minutes later, Casey came out for me.

We entered directly upon a living room. It was sparsely furnished but it was clean. The frowning woman came up to me at once. She stretched out a hand and we shook. She said, "I'm Alice Trenton." Her hand was large and hard and bony and scaly-dry.

Casey said, "My friend, Peter Chambers. Mr. Fred Davis, and Mrs. Davis—Auntie."

The man in the wheel chair blinked his eyes.

The round little woman wearing the heavy dark glasses said, "Won't you sit down, Mr. Chambers?"

"Thank you."

Mary Davis was small and round and apple-cheeked. Her white hair was worn high on her head and kept in place by many blond bobby pins. When she smiled, her cheeks dimpled. Her teeth were small and white and her skin was unwrinkled. She wore a simple tan dress with a thin brown leather belt around the middle. She had a peculiar, hushed, hesitant manner of speaking, the tone just above a whisper. It was as though she were speaking of sacred things plus the fact that there was a light sleeper in the next room whom she did not wish to awaken. Mary Davis was a sweet-looking middle-aged woman with no special distinction. Place her in a crowded suburban supermarket on a busy afternoon, and she would blend; it would be difficult to discover her. Except for the hugh dark-glass spectacles. They created a shock effect, totally incongruous with the commonplace orderliness of Mary Davis. It made for the destruction of the illusion of the prosaic. It was as though her tongue were protruding or her dress had a scarlet patch at the lower rear or one breast was hanging out.

Fred Davis. He sat in a corner of the room, utterly motionless in his wheel chair. He wore clean white trousers and clean white sneakers and a clean white sport shirt opened to a deep V on his bare chest. There was sparse grey curly hair on his chest and sparse grey wispy hair on his head. His face was thin and white-pale, a long face with a long nose and deep lines in the thin cheeks. Loose flesh in crêpe-like pouches hung beneath his chin. His hands dangled from the arms of the chair, the fingers shiny from disuse. Only his eyes were alive: darting-bright, moving, following the talk.

Mary Davis touched Casey's arm, and smiled at me again. "It's like a miracle . . . a real miracle . . . I . . . I can hardly believe it."

Alice Trenton said: "Got work to do. Washing. Please

excuse me, folks." She rubbed the palms of her hands along the sides of her dress, bowed awkwardly, waved small, and went through a door toward the rear of the house.

Casey lit a cigarette. "Mr. Chambers," he said, "is a detective."

Auntie said: "Detective?"

"It's about Pop."

"Oh." There was a handkerchief folded in a neat square on a corner of a table. She lifted it, went across to her husband, patted his forehead with it and wiped away a sliver of drool that escaped from a corner of his mouth. Then she came back to us. She said, "Please sit down, Mr. Chambers. You too, Casey." She tapped the table. "Right here. Please sit down."

We pulled up chairs and sat.

I said, "Is it all right if we talk about it? About Henry Moore?"

She stood over us. She didn't answer. She said, "May I get you something cool? Iced tea?"

Casey said, "Don't bother, Auntie."

"No bother. No bother at all." She went out the same door Alice Trenton had gone.

Casey looked at me and I looked at Casey and the speechless man in the corner looked at both of us. Mary Davis came back with a tray of drinks. She set a glass in front of me and one in front of Casey. There was another glass with a teaspoon. She went with that to Fred Davis. Carefully, she ladled iced tea into his mouth. Then she wiped his mouth with the handkerchief, returned to us, put down the glass and spoon on the table. She said, "And you of the police, Mr. Chambers?"

Casey said, "No. He's a private detective. He's helping me to find out—about Pop."

"Why?"

"I don't understand, Auntie."

"Why stir it up? He's dead."

"But he's dead as a thief and a murderer. Pop wasn't—"

"He's dead. We can't bring him back."

"But if . . . if I can prove that he wasn't what they say he was . . . a little bit . . . somehow . . . I'd be satisfied."

We couldn't see her eyes behind the dark glasses. She was silent, a fingernail tapping the teaspoon on the table. Then, in her soft hushed voice she said, "You're a good boy, Casey. You always were good . . . since you were a little boy. You're right. Of course you're right."

I said, "Is there anything you know? About any of it?"

"I think so."

I turned toward Fred Davis, turned back. "Is it all right if we discuss this, any aspect of it, in front of Mr. Davis?"

"Certainly."

I wished I could see her eyes. How can you talk with a person whose eyes you cannot see? There is no feel, no intimacy, no tie. It is as though a conversation by megaphone is being bellowed across an empty space.

It popped before I could restrain it. I said, "Is there a reason why you wear sun glasses indoors?"

Silence. An odd uncomfortable silence. Then her hand moved up and she snapped off the glasses. The only sound in the room was Casey's gasp.

One eye seemed frozen in its socket. It was wide, rigid and glaring, the upper lid wrinkled-stiff and inflamed. Palpably it was sightless, pale blue and like shattered glass, giving back no reflection. The other eye was fixed on Casey's empty sleeve and it was wet with tears. She said, "I shall be totally blind by next year."

Casey said, "No."

She smiled as she put the glasses back over her eyes. Her voice was exactly as it was before, quiet and hushed and unemotional. "I don't know what will become of us, Fred in his chair and me without eyes. It will be too much for Alice, far too much."

"Something . . ." Casey said. "There must be something. You've been to doctors, haven't you?"

"To the doctors I could afford."

"And what did they say?"

"What I can't afford. There's a great man up in Boston, a famous man. Dr. Blake took me to see him. You remember Dr. Blake, Casey?"

"Remember him since I was knee-high to nothing."

"He took me to Boston. About a year ago. Before the one eye became blind. It all happened just as the doctor said it would. There's still a chance now, even that the one eye is gone."

"But . . . if they knew . . . why didn't they do something?"

"Because it costs fifteen thousand dollars. Fifteen thousand dollars for a series of operations and the necessary care afterward."

"And your sight can still be saved?"

"Yes. Only one eye now but who needs more than one eye? Except . . . we don't have fifteen thousand dollars, and these things simply aren't done by charity. It's not just the surgeon's fees, it's a whole series of treatments after that. You're in a hospital for two and a half months."

Something hit me. "A year ago, you say?"

"Yes."

"This have anything to do . . . with what happened to Mr. Moore?"

"I think so."

"Will you tell us about it, Mrs. Davis?"

"Yes, I will. Do you know about Henry and Fred and myself?"

Casey said, "I told him everything."

"Henry was good, gracious and fine." She smiled, dimpling. "He practically lived with us, with Fred and myself and Fred loved him as I did. He was our brother. But years ago"—the smiles came again—"I was a pretty woman, and a timid one . . . I still am timid. What with Fred, an invalid husband and Henry, a fine, good-looking man, there was bound to be gossip. We cured that, bit by bit, informing people that Henry was my brother. And brother indeed he was."

"Yes, Casey told me about it."

Her shoulders humped in a shrug. "I was cowardly perhaps but we can't all be strong. Public opinion, the opinion of my neighbors . . . that sort of thing is important to little people, to people like Fred and myself, and to Henry too, for that matter. He wouldn't have done a thing ever, to place Fred or myself in an improper light."

"Of course not, Mrs. Davis."

"I want it absolutely understood that there was nothing wrong in our relationship. I want that clear as crystal. I'm not that kind of woman and Henry was not that kind of man." She went with the handkerchief to Fred and patted his face. She said, "Would you bring me a chair here, Casey, please? I'd like to sit beside Fred as I talk."

Casey brought a chair, and Mary Davis sat near Fred.

I said, "About Henry Moore . . . ?"

"You can imagine," she said, "how Fred and I felt when I came back from Boston with Dr. Blake. And you can imagine, I am sure, how Henry felt. In a way, he seemed more distraught then either Fred or myself. I suppose that was because he was always the active one, he shouldered so many of our burdens. We talked for hours and hours . . . but there simply was no solution."

"And then . . . ?" Casey said.

"Your father had an idea. He knew a man . . . the man had been a depositor in the bank where your father worked many years ago. Your father had been a customer of his when the man had owned a quiet little club, also many years ago. They had had many conversations over the bar, knew a good deal about each other, their philosophies, their ideas, the inner thoughts that men express in a quiet and convivial atmosphere."

"How many years ago?" I said. "Would you know?"

"A long time. Henry hadn't seen this man in perhaps twenty years. But we were in a crisis . . . and it was a case of any port in a storm. The man had grown to great riches and Henry decided to go and see him."

"For what?"

"For a loan. We figured it out carefully. Henry had reapplied for a job at the bank, and they were glad to have him back. The job including occasional overtime, paid ninety dollars a week. Of that, sixty dollars each week would go to paying off the loan. Plus, Fred and I would move into Henry's house in Queens, thus cutting our expenses, and, from Fred's compensation, we would add another twenty-five dollars a week. Thus, within four years, the loan would be paid off."

"I see."

"It didn't leave us much to live on, but we were all getting on in years and we felt, somehow, we could manage. And there was another consideration."

"What was that?"

"Casey. Casey was listed as dead. This was a year ago. I don't know much about these things but sooner or later, there would be money coming to Henry from the government, a matter of Casey's policy, something like that. When and if that came, it would be applied to paying off the loan so much more quickly."

"I understand."

"We planned it all very carefully before Henry went to the man for the loan. It was a form of an appeal in an emergency to a rich man. We prayed that it would work. Henry called the man and, on the morning of May 10th, he went to him."

"That's a year ago?"

"Yes."

"Where was the appointment for?"

"The man's office and the appointment was for nine o'clock. At nine-thirty, Henry called us. He told me, over the phone, that he had had his conference and that the man told him to come back at noontime."

"And then?"

"At three o'clock Henry came to my apartment in the Bronx. He appeared thoughtful but not discouraged. He said there was a great possibility that he would be able to get the fifteen thousand dollars, but not as a loan."

"Not . . . as a loan?"

"He said that he'd been offered a piece of work and that he could *earn* the money that we so desperately needed . . . and that, actually the request for a *loan* had been turned down."

"What kind of work?"

"He didn't tell us. It was a terribly hot day and I could see that he was extremely nervous. He was perspiring and mopping himself and saying that he had to leave, that he had an appointment. Finally, I told him to take a shower and change, that he looked all wilted. He always kept a change of clothing up there."

"And . . . ?"

"He did that, and he left. I remember that last moment so distinctly. He went to Fred and patted Fred's face and said, 'Wish me luck.' Then, gravely, he shook hands with me . . . and I never saw Henry Moore again in my life."

"What?"

"The next we knew is what we read in the papers."

I dragged my eyes away from her. I sipped my iced tea which was now warm. I lit a cigarette. I said, "Whom did he go to for that loan? What was the man's name?"

"Edward Adams."

I shoved out of my chair and went to her. I said as kindly as I could: "You knew that that was the man's house which, allegedly, he had attempted to rob and where, allegedly, he had committed a murder. Edward Adams. You must have known that from the newspapers. That's a fact, isn't it?"

"Yes."

"Then why didn't you go to the police?"

"How do you know I didn't?"

"Because I've seen the police files. There's absolutely no mention of you or your husband."

She turned, patted Fred's face with the handkerchief, then put a corner beneath her glasses and wiped her eye. "You want to know why I didn't go to the police. Is that it?"

"Yes."

"There were two reasons, one personal, one practical. I talked it over with Fred and Fred agreed with me." She turned toward him, smiled, turned back to me, unsmiling. "Oh, Fred and I can talk. He can blink his eyes—one for yes, and two for no. We talk all the time."

"What were the reasons, Mrs. Davis?"

"The first, as I said, was personal. If I went to the police, our whole story would come out. Henry Moore was our friend for eighteen years. We ended any possible gossip when we decided to tell people he was my brother. Now it would all come out. That he was not my brother at all. How would it look? What would people think? What would they say? And he was dead, dead . . . we couldn't bring him back. And his son was dead. What purpose would be served? We couldn't help him. All we could do . . . would be further harm."

"How so, Mrs. Davis?"

"If we could have helped, of course I would have gone to the police, despite myself and Fred and any scandal. But how could we help? All we could do was add fuel to the fire. We could give them motive, that we could do and nothing else. Between us we know that in his desperation, he had just gone crazy. We felt that once the loan had been turned down, he had decided to . . . to . . ."

Casey said, "Of course, of course, Auntie."

"We felt he had just gone crazy, that he had decided to get that money one way or another . . . and then when the woman had appeared, the man's wife, Henry in his panic . . ."

Casey came to me and said, "Thanks, fella."

"For what?"

"For tracking it down, and getting it over with. At least now I can understand it. At least now it's not . . . not impossible. Okay. Finished. You'll get a bill to me and you'll be paid for your work."

I looked for an ashtray, and flattened my cigarette. I said, "I'm not so sure."

"Not so sure . . . of what?"

"That's it's finished."

"But why?"

"That's what I'd like to ask . . . why? According to Captain Weaver and all the statements in the police file, Henry Moore was a stranger to every one of the parties involved, from the murdered woman to the witness, Matthew Bennett, to the husband Edward Adams. Eddie Adams denied knowing Henry Moore, said he was a complete stranger. Why?"

Hope flickered in his old eyes. "Yes. Why?"

"If Eddie Adams had told the police the story Mrs. Davis just old us—or that part of the story with which he was involved—it would have been perfect. A man comes for a loan, he's turned down, he's desperate, he decides to steal. That linked with what Mrs. Davis just told us, and I would have agreed with you—it would be finished. But not one word of any of this turns up in the police files, plus Eddie Adams flatly denies any knowledge of Henry Moore, and that's also in the police files . . ."

"What do we do, Pete?"

"We keep punching, that's what we do. What've we got to lose? Mrs. Davis."

"Yes?"

"You said that he'd taken a shower and changed his clothes."

"That's right."

"Which means that one set of clothing remained. Do you have these clothes?"

"No."

"You've disposed of them?"

"No. I mean I don't have them here. My sister, when she learned of my eye trouble, insisted that we move down here. When we decided to do that, I packed the things we didn't need into a little trunk and left it up there."

"In the Bronx?"

"Yes. In the basement storage room of the house in which we had our apartment. The superintendent took care of it. If ever we thought we wanted it, we would send for it."

"What was your address in the Bronx?"

"12 Horner Avenue."

"And the super's name?"

"Mr. Gilbert."

"And is there a key to the trunk?"

"Yes."

"May I have it?"

She looked toward Casey and Casey nodded. She said, "Just a moment," left the room, returned with the key, and gave it to me.

"Thank you. And now I think it's time I ran along."

"Please. Won't you stay and have a bite with us?"

"No, thank you. I'm sure Casey'd like that, though."

Casey grinned. "You kiddin'? I'm already committed. Why don't you stick around too?"

"No, thanks. I'll see you back at the hotel later. Goodbye Mr. Davis, Mrs. Davis, my respects to your sister. And Case, I'll take care of the reservations so that we fly back this evening."

But weather set in. Paradise blew up. Rain came down like the seas had turned over and the planes were grounded. We were holed up at the Empress overnight, no reduction in prices, and we got off the ground bright and early next morning, sun shining bravely and natives walking around with faces that said that any unfortunate mention of rain was distinctly a fraud. We landed at La Guardia at one o'clock and at two o'clock I was back in the cubicle of the tailor shop waiting for my one suit to be pressed and freshened.

At the Montero, I watched Casey's reflection in the mirror as he shaved and I voiced admiration of his dexterity. Lips ringed with lather, he said: "When do we go to the Bronx?"

"Let you know in a minute."

I used the phone for Jane Rawlings. Jane was home and I told her I was home. "Good," she said. "Cocktails?"

"But what else? Where?"

"The Drake. And the sooner the better."

"I'm ready now, Janie m'love. Half hour?"

"You talked me into it."

I hung up and I embraced Casey, then I looked at my watch. "About four-thirty all right for the Bronx?"

"Sure. Where you heading for now?"

"Cocktails. With a lady."

"Same lady you interviewed the other night?"

"Yep." I kissed him on the forehead. "I'm in love."

"Real quick."

"That's me. Quick. Both ways. Fall in, fall out." I rubbed a hand through his hair. "Keep loose, kid. I'll pick you up later."

The lounge of the Drake was lovely with wallpaper and romantic with music piped by wire. My lady was wrapped within a charcoal-grey man-tailored suit with a high-necked pink blouse, but man-tailoring or no, my lady was all woman, and every man in the near-enough vicinity was acutely conscious of that. Her hair was combed in a tousled upsweep, and she said, almost breathlessly, as soon as I'd sat down beside her: "How's with the tuxedo?"

"No." I groaned. "We don't start that again."

She turned down the corners of her mouth. "It'll keep. Talk. Today I'm completely cooperative."

I hesitated a moment. "About your father . . . I'm sorry about the other night . . ."

"Just a minute."

"Sure."

Her black eyes turned on me, and dropped. "We all try so hard to be modern, and zippy, and new-fashioned, but sometimes . . . we just don't make it."

"Sure."

The eyes came up again. "My father died as all people

must. He lived a full, long life. Miss him? I miss him like all hell. But I don't believe in public displays of grief. And I don't believe in widow's weeds and protracted weepings. I was taught to live life and live it quick and live it full. So I think I acted up a little bit the other night, and *I'm* sorry. I've said my piece and I hope it makes a mite of sense to you. Now what do you want to know about my Dad?"

"You know I'm a private detective."

She smiled. "Sounds absolutely detestable."

"I'm working on a thing that involves a former partner of your father's. Eddie Adams. Know him?"

"I've met him. Several times."

"May I ask some questions? Part of business?"

"Ask away, detective."

"Were you acquainted at all with your father's business affairs?"

"More than 'acquainted at all.' My dad was a great guy. And I was an only child and my mother's been dead for many years. He always talked to me, sounded me out on things."

"Know anything about the Stardust Room?"

"Yes."

"How'd your father and Adams get together on that deal?"

The waiter came and I ordered Scotch and water and Jane wanted green créme de menthe on shaved ice. The waiter made his notations on his pad and went away. Jane said, "My father had been in the restaurant business all his life, owned chains in almost every big city in the country. As he grew older, the active management got to be a little too much for him and he believed in active, personal management."

"So?"

"Bit by bit, he disposed of his holdings and after a while he was virtually retired—but it didn't take."

"Rarely does, unless you're sick or senile."

"He wasn't senile, but there was a complication. His heart was kicking up. Yet, he was sort of casting about for a one-shot deal that would interest him, keep him occupied, but wouldn't overload him. That's when Mr. Adams got to him."

"About the Stardust?"

"It was in its vague talking stage at the time. Adams conceived the idea of a night club on a grand scale over in Jersey. What with Dad's experience in the restaurant business and Adams' in the night club business, they were a natural combination. The Diamond Circle was on its last legs at the time. My father investigated the Jersey proposition."

"Were they supposed to go in as partners?"

"No. Adams wanted Dad to make the full investment."

"So?"

"Experts delivered their estimates, there was a lot of chatter but it boiled down to a half million bucks. Dad could afford it but he didn't want to bear the brunt of exclusive ownership with Adams having a goodly chunk as active manager and idea man. Dad made him a counter proposition—that they go in as full partners. each investing half the money, and each putting in full time as active managers."

"Was that during the time Adams was winding up the Diamond Circle?"

"Exactly that time. He was worth, oh perhaps a hundred thousand dollars in cash which wasn't enough, but he was digging up the rest—he needed a quarter of a million to go in as full partner. Then he got into his own personal troubles, what with the death of his wife up there, but they finally straightened out their deal as full partners and the Stardust Room was born."

"But after a while your father backed out, didn't he?"

"He didn't back out. He was bought out. The gambling thing began, and Dad wouldn't take any of that. As soon as the conferences were set up with the hoodlums and the pseudo-politicos—Dad insisted on out, and, as a matter of fact, Adams was glad to get rid of him. Once the gambling entered into it, the thing was virtually a gold mine, so what did he need Dad for? Adams paid him off, honestly, to the penny and in quick time. Anything else, Mr. Detective?"

"Nope. That's about it."

"Have I helped?"

"I don't know."

She looked at me curiously. "You people always work like that?"

"We've got all kinds of systems."

"Well, now, about that tuxedo . . ."

The waiter brought our drinks. I sipped Scotch but Jane Rawlings grinned over the green glass. "About that tuxedo . . ."

"What's the production this time?"

"Real fancy ball tonight. Charity affair at the Waldorf. Tickets all paid for. The nicest people. I'm looking forward to it."

"But I've got work to do, Sweetie."

"I hate people who call me Sweetie."

"So do I. But . . . I've got work this evening."

"Work. Work your head off. We don't start till late. I don't want you to call for me before midnight. Things don't begin to come to life before then."

"You're for me."

"And then there's going to be a party at Ichabod Rally's place. You know Rally?"

"I do."

"Then you know his parties. All right, Peter?" She looked at her watch. "Got to go now. I've an appointment at the dressmaker's. Let's have dinner together and talk more. Dinner, early. Six or seven. Can you make it?"

"I don't know. I'll try. I'll call you."

"And try and do something about a tuxedo." She slanted a glance at me, up-long. "You allowed to go home yet?"

"Not yet."

"I don't understand."

"It's a long story."

I signalled the waiter for my check, fumbled in my wallet, and just about made it. Now I grabbed a glance at my watch and I pushed back my chair. Jane said, "What's *your* hurry?"

"Got to make the bank."

"Well, wait for me."

"Come on."

Outside, she clung to my arm, turned me toward her and widened her black eyes. "Try and make it for dinner."

"You be at your phone."

I broke for a cab and she wailed after me, prompting a large and knowing wink from the cab driver:

"And do something about the tuxedo."

The cab waited, while I made the bank at the usual split second before the doors ground closed. I cashed a check, bemoaned the fact as to how money flies, came out into the street, got locked into my cab again and was driven uptown to my car. I gassed up and oiled up and watered up and aired up, and then I pulled up in front of the Montero and went in and used the house phone for Casey. I was early but he was ready and minutes later we were wheeling up the West Side Highway en route to the Bronx. We swung off at 181st, went East along Featherbed Lane, across to Tremont, and on toward Horner Avenue. I made a sharp left turn and Casey's body leaned against me. I said, "What's the lump?"

"Lump?" All innocence.

I tapped him. There was steel inside his jacket pocket.

"No lump?" I said.

"Oh that? It's the Luger."

"What for? We're going up to look at a trunk. What do you expect to find in it?"

He shrugged. "I don't know."

"Don't tell me you're going melodramatic on me."

"Happens. When you buddy up with a detective."

Horner Avenue was in a crowded section of the Bronx, contiguous tenements alive with activity, garbage cans lining the edges of the sidewalks, cars double-parked, stoops a forum for housewives, streets teeming with kids, and open windows filled with mamas half-hanging out with their crossed arms as cushions.

I parked the car and we walked to 12 Horner Avenue. An alley running along the side of the house bore a rusted metal sign stating: SUPER. The alley opened to a narrow court with two doors. One door had small stencilled printing: SUPERINTENDENT. The other door had a handprinted-amateur sign tacked to it: BASEMENT. KEEP OUT. The superintendent's door had a push button and I pushed it. We could hear a bell ringing inside and the answering wild barking of a dog but nobody opened the door. I tried the basement door and it gave on the turn of the knob.

"Let's look," I said.

The place was littered with baby carriages, bicycles, broken washing machines, old stoves, rotting cabinets and ancient refrigerators. Whatever was moveable was chained down. But there were no trunks. There was another door in the rear, half open, with a stairway leading down. I said, "I'll take a gander down there. You'd better hang around outside."

"Why?"

"In case the super shows. I don't want him to think he's had an attack of marauders. You explain it. Do you know him?"

"Never saw him in my life but you're the boss." He went out and I could hear his heels resounding along the stone of the alley.

I pushed open the door of the subcellar. The stairway had a steep angle and it ended in complete blackness. There was no bannister. I went down carefully, feeling my way, holding one hand against the damp roughness of the side wall. When I reached bottom I couldn't see in front of me. It was cool, almost cold, and a thin veil of cobweb brushed against my face. I turned my head and looked up the stairway. The upper door had swung back to its half open position, a silver of dim light palely illuminating the top portion of the stairway. I turned back to blackness. I ran my hand along the inner wall for a light switch and finally I found it and clicked it. High up, a naked yellow bulb was a candle in the distance.

It was an enormous subcellar, jagged blocks of stone making up the ceiling and the walls. It was damp, damp-odorous, cobwebby and silent, no sound from the street filtering through. The single bulb, strung on a wire and hanging from the middle, threw an eerie lemon light amongst the shadows. Most of the sub-cellar was empty, meters and fuse boxes along the walls. The uneven stone floor was wet and a large red-brown water beetle, antennae glinting, scurried from the light into the periphery of darkness. Toward the rear, tarpaulins covered a serried hill of bulky objects. I shuddered once and I went to work.

I pulled off the tarpaulin, disclosing mildewed trunks and brown paper bundles and cord-wrapped suitcase. I tried my key and when I found the trunk it fitted, I pulled the trunk into the light and opened it. It didn't contain much: a man's brown suit, a blue striped suit, underwear, three white shirts, two ties, two pairs of brown socks, a few items of bent and tarnished silverware and a broken electric clock. I looked through the striped suit first. It held nothing except a discolored dime. The brown suit had nothing except a folded letter in an inner pocket of the jacket. I unfolded the letter. The stationery was small, neat and expensive. Engraved on top was: Fletcher Lewis, M.D., 750 Fifth Avenue, New York. Written beneath that was the date, April 28th, and the following:

> "Dear Mr. Adams, I am sorry to be compelled to inform you that, as consultant, I agree with your other physicians that Mrs. Adams has a pulmonary condition which is inoperable. I also agree with the prognosis. Her condition is critical. You ask how long? I would say she cannot last more than eight weeks. I hope I am wrong but I do not think I am. As a matter of fact my prognosis is more optimistic than that of either of your other physicians. You asked for it straight from the shoulder. I am sorry but that is it." It was signed: "Fletcher Lewis."

A little bell rang in my head, and then another little bell but they didn't have time to go to gongs. I looked up from the letter—and Olga Adams was opposite me.

She wore a blue suit and flat-heeled blue shoes and most of her hair was beneath a blue beret. There was a small grin on her face and a small gun in her hand. She was quite near me. Too near. But she wasn't a professional. She said, "This place is perfect."

"For what?"

"For your demise. Real quiet down here. A shot wouldn't be heard. Suits me fine. You know how allergic I am to publicity."

Also she talked too much. That wasn't professional either. It gave me an opportunity to inch closer. "You wouldn't dare," I said. It was corny, but it gave me another step forward and I was within reach. As her gun hand moved outward, my left slapped down on it and my right met her jaw in a jolt. She dropped like the floor had been pulled from under her. I was stooping for the little gun when the voice said: "I wouldn't do that if I was you. I wouldn't do nuthin' but stand up straight."

I stood up straight, the little gun remaining on the floor. Frankie Gold was at the foot of the stairway, a large gun in his very professional hand. He said, "Surprised, fink?"

"Twice surprised."

"The little lady's got a lot of brains under that blonde hair."

"How'd you get here?"

"That's what I'm beginning to tell you, fink." His thin grin spread. "Brains. She figured we got you tied up by your house and we got you tied up by your office—but you don't show in either spot. She figures you got to eat, and she figures you need dough to eat, and where is the dough kept at? So she calls on Frankie and we check where your bank is, and that's where we park out, me and her. You show up and the rest is a tail job. The little lady wanted the pleasure but it looks like she muffed it. I won't. G'bye, fink."

I tried for more talk but Frankie had run out of words. His arm came out, straight and level, and I saw his finger tighten on the trigger and I heard the shot billowing back from the walls, hollowly. I waited to drop but I didn't drop. Frankie Gold dropped, blood bursting from the side of his head, the gun clattering to the stone of the floor.

Casey Moore stepped over him and came into the cellar.

Dryly he said, "Me and my Luger. Melodramatic."

"My apologies, and my blessings." I moved to Frankie and bent over him but Frankie was all gone. I got up and said, "Casey, where'd you drop from, and thank heaven you did?"

"From the middle of the stairway."

"How'd you get there?"

"Well, I'm upstairs waiting for the super as you instructed

me. I notice this car parked, with this guy and the lady inside, and they both seem to be having an eye on me, so I scram."

"How?"

"I go to the corner, hail a cab and drive off."

"Where to?"

"Around the block. When I get out, I've got the jump on them. The lady's already gone. Me, I'm watching a hallway. This guy's outside the alleyway. He takes one look around and slips in. It doesn't take long before I slip in after him. You can figure the rest."

"Where were you when she was talking to me?"

"Right behind him, about twelve steps up. He's at the foot of the stairway, with a bead on you, listening. I'm on top of him, with a bead on him. Who pegs whom first becomes a matter of judgment. I'm glad it worked out."

Nervously I said, "So am I."

He looked toward Olga. "How's the lady?"

I bent and examined. "Sleeping peacefully." I looked past her, thought a moment, said, "This tomb is practically sound-proof and a good thing. But let's get this stuff in place and get out of here." I stood up. "Give me a hand."

I closed the trunk, moved the other trunks and bundles and suitcases together, shoved our trunk into place, and Casey helped me with the tarpaulin.

Olga Adams began to move. I let her. I picked up her little pistol and watched her. She sat up. I pointed the thing at her. Now *she* said it: "You wouldn't dare."

"Of course I wouldn't."

She stood up, touched the point of her chin gingerly, dusted herself off, looked about, saw Frankie, opened her eyes wide, then opened her mouth wider to scream.

"Don't," I said. It stopped her. I said: "He's dead."

She looked about wildly, ran toward the stairs. Casey grabbed her arm and she flung about. I got to them and her mouth opened to scream again. I closed it. With a short jab to the same point of her jaw. She sagged against Casey. I said, "It's not the noise I'm worried about. I just don't want her to start getting hysterical."

Casey said, "What now?"

"Where's their car?"

"Right in front of the alley."

"Who was driving?"

"She was."

I looked in her pockets and found the car keys. I said, "You got a clean handkerchief, Case?"

He leaned her against me, found a handkerchief, and showed it to me. It was large, and that was excellent. I said, "Shake it out and fold it into a bandage sort of thing. Like you were going to bind a wound . . ."

"Sure."

He did it, handed it over, and I passed it around her head and tied it over her eyes. Casey said, "I get it. Something wrong with her eyes, somebody's got to lead her."

"Right." I gave him her car keys and I gave him mine. "You go up first. Open her car and get the motor running, and leave the door open for me. Then get into my car and be ready to follow me."

"Roger."

He went up. I gave him a few moments, then lifted her and carried her up. In the alley, I set her on her feet, put my arm around her, and half-carried her, half-walked her out to the street. I got her into the car without too much trouble. A couple of the loiterers stared, but I was helping a woman who had trouble with her eyes and I didn't give them much opportunity to stare. I ran around to the driver's seat, slammed the doors, shifted the gear, and we were rolling. A glance at the rear view showed me Casey behind me. We rode north until we reached Van Cortlandt Park. I parked where it was isolated and removed the handkerchief from her eyes. She stirred uneasily. I looked in the rear view. Casey was parked about fifty feet back.

She was slumped down in the seat, and now I pulled her up. I slapped at her face, until she came to. "Wha . . . ?" she said. "Wha . . . ?" I kept slapping, gently. Finally, she was awake, her face strangely childlike again, the expression innocent and frightened.

"Hi," I said. I reached into my pocket and brought out her little gun. I slapped out the bullets and threw them far out into the grass of the park. I said, "Here's your gun. Between you and me, I think you're a little nuts. Stop playing games with yourself."

She didn't touch the gun. She said, "Frankie . . . ?"

"He's very dead."

She gasped and her face whitened. I moved her over, opened the glove compartment , threw in the gun and snapped it shut. "Look," I said, "go home, and stay home. Will you do that, please? Let dear old Eddie operate, and you butt out. Stay home and be a lady. Or are you looking for headlines? Big, black ones?"

"What are you up to? What are you up to, anyway?"

"You're going to know soon enough. I'm coming to the end of the line. In the meantime, go home and stay home. Okay?"

She was silent.

I said, "Frankie's dead. You could have been dead. Stop playing movies. Go home and shut up, and so will I. I didn't see you today. Neither did my pal. You were out for a drive, period. You don't know a thing about Frankie Gold. Like that you're all the way in the clear. It's my idea you like to play movies but you're not a bad kid. That's my idea. Make me look smart. Okay?"

Silence again. Then she said, "Yes."

I opened the door and moved out of the driver's seat. She shoved over and then, very faintly, she said, "Thanks."

"Forget it."

The car shot forward. I watched it until it was out of sight. Then I went to Casey. I said, "I don't know whether I mentioned it before. Eddie Adams has a wife named Olga. That was Olga. You never saw Olga today. As far as you're concerned, you don't know nuthin' from no Olgas." I winked and crooked my mouth up. "Check?"

"You're the boss."

"Switch it off and come on out."

He shut off the motor, came out and gave me the car key. We walked deep into the park. There was nobody near. I said, "Give me the gun."

"Why?"

"Because I don't want you mixed up in this, that's why. This is my kind of work and I know how to handle it. Fork it over."

He gave it to me and I pointed it upward and blasted at the sky.

"What's that for?" Casey said.

"For the record."

"I don't get it."

I showed him my palm. "In there."

"What?"

"Cordite particles, invisible to the eye, but they show up under certain police tests. I shot the gun."

"*You* did?"

"Yeah. Me, In self-defense. He's a murderous hoodlum and the cops'll be glad to be rid of him. But if it comes to a check, I want it to check."

"But there's only one bullet in him, two bullets discharged from the gun, and no second bullet around."

"So what? A bullet could have been shot from this Luger at any time before now."

"And where'd you get the gun?"

"Borrowed it from you. You're a client. I couldn't go home or to the office, and I needed protection, and you had this Luger, was souvenir, so I borrowed it from you."

"And who gets this story?"

"That I don't know—yet."

"And why the closed mouth about the little lady?"

"A kid living in a jazzed-up dream world. But she got a bellyful this afternoon. She saw the real thing happen and you saw what it did to her. Dream world, movie-heroine, only married a short time to mister big shot. Doesn't know a thing because a guy like Eddie Adams doesn't figure to let her in on anything. That's a doll to keep around the house, and use when necessary. Anyway, I figured you and I'd give the kid a break. Any objections?"

"No."

We got into the car, returned to civilization, and stopped at the first drug store. I called Police Headquarters, said, "There's a dead man in the basement of 12 Horner Avenue," and hung up.

Back at the Montero, I called the office of Dr. Fletcher Lewis. I was informed that the doctor's evening office hours were from seven to nine. I asked for an appointment and received one for seven-thirty. I made more calls, three in all, to various doctors with who I was acquainted. I learned that Dr. Fletcher Lewis was a specialist, high in his profession, and a man of irreproachable ethics. I called Jane Rawlings.

"Hi," she said.

"How about dinner?"

"A likely thought. Where and when?"

"When . . . right away. Where . . . hold it a minute." I wanted a place not too far away from 750 Fifth Avenue. La Maison Rouge was at 61st and Fifth. I said, "French?"

"Always."

"Maison Rouge?"

"Fine. Meet you at the bar. Bet I get there first."

She didn't.

I got there first.

Lawrence, the maître d', said, "You wish to order now, Mr. Chambers? While you wait for the lady?"

I ordered, and a table in the rear was spread while I waited at the bar. I'd finished half of a Rob Roy when Jane showed up, elegant in a tight black beaded dress with a small mink jacket. "Beautiful," I said.

"You too." Her teeth shone in a grin.

"Let's go where it's romantic. I've already ordered."

"You're for me."

The rear room of Maison Rouge had maroon velvet walls, and gold tapestries, and faraway dim pink lights, and each table had a candle encased in a frosted soft pink spiral of glass. At a distance there was mellow music from a harp and when the harp music ceased, there was a muted violin. Lawrence had selected a corner table for us and we sat side by side and thigh-close. Jane removed the little jacket, revealing lush and warm-glowing depths, and she revealed more as she bent over and kissed the lobe of my ear. "You're for me," she said. "You worked out the early dinner real fine. Did you work out the tuxedo too?"

"Murder," I said.

"What keeps you from home?"

"Not now. Let's relax now. Let's chat. Let's know about each other."

The dinner was wonderful, slow and long, and we talked all through it. Over the demitasse and brandy, I said, "I've an appointment at seven-thirty."

"I don't care about seven-thirty. How about midnight?"

"I think I'll be able to make it."

"With tuxedo?"

"I'm going to try."

"Now that that's out of the way—what's at seven-thirty?"

"Business."

"Really? Can I come? I've never seen a detective at work."

"If you've got nothing else to do . . ."

"I'll tell you what I've got to do, my fine-feathered friend. The dressmaker's to deliver a dress, but that's all right, the downstairs man has instructions to accept it. Then at eight-thirty from Elizabeth Varden, the one and only Georgette shows up. Georgette, she makes me beautiful. And then at nine-thirty, a wonderful man from Paris, Henri Daniel, with the most divine jewelry. So, I'm free until approximately eight-thirty."

"Be my guest."

We presented ourselves at the offices of Dr. Fletcher Lewis at seven-thirty. We were shown into his consulting room. Dr. Lewis was a small man with a trim white beard, fluffy white hair, and an engaging tobacco-stained smile. I said, "I'm Peter Chambers. The lady is my wife."

I got a pinch for that, surreptitious but soft and the doctor bowed. "Beautiful lady," he said. Then, more business-like, "My secretary informs me that you're not here as a patient."

"That's right, sir. I'm investigating a matter for the Coronet Insurance Company, and I'm here to enlist your help."

The doctor said, "Won't you sit down, Mrs. Chambers?"

"Thank you."

He turned to me. "I'll help, if I can. But please remember that any information regarding a physician and patient is an absolutely privileged matter, completely confidential, even in a court of law."

"I'm aware of that, doctor. I'd simply like to know whether at any time, you had a patient by name Dorothy Adams?"

He went to a cabinet, riffled through a card-index file. I waited, fumbling with some of his stationery neatly stacked on a corner of his desk. Finally, his head came up from the file. He said, "No."

"While you're there, doctor. Was a Mr. Edward Adams a patient of yours?"

He didn't look to the file. "Yes. Haven't seen him for a long time, though. Perhaps a year."

"When, exactly, doctor? When did he last visit you? Could I have the date and time?" Dr. Fletcher Lewis frowned, an expression of doubt wrinkling across his face. Hurriedly, I said, "I don't want to know a thing about his illness or the treatment or the advice. None of the privileged communications. Just the date and time. There's no violation of any medical confidence in that information, and it might be vitally important to us."

He thought a moment and then the frown smoothed out. He said, "I believe that's quite correct." He bent to the card-index, fingered cards, pushed one back and read from it. "May 10th, last," he said. "Ten-thirty, A.M."

"Thank you." The little bell began to ring in my head.

"Is there something else?"

"No, sir. You've been very kind and very helpful. Thank you again and good evening to you."

"And a very good evening to you, young man. Delighted to have met you, Mrs. Chambers."

Outside, Jane Rawlings lifted her eyebrows and intoned: "That's work?"

"Go home now, dear wife."

"Midnight, husband?"

"I hope. Keep a lamp in the window."

I put her into a cab and then I was a parade on Fifth Avenue, by myself. Many bells were now ringing in my head but indiscriminately, the sequence as disordered as an ashtray at a poker game. It was imperative that I go home. Home, the bells could begin to chime a melody with meaning: home was the baton, home the maestro, home the music and the orchestration. I had to go home. But how?

I pondered that on my parade on Fifth Avenue. The house had a front entrance and a rear entrance. Eddie Adams' hatchet boys were playing sentinel there, front and back. How would I get in? I thought of disguise and quickly dismissed it. Disguise. Dark glasses. A beard. A lump on my shoulder and a cane and a bent over walk. None of it would work. Eddie's boys weren't amateurs. They probably knew me—I'm well-known in my town, especially to the hard boys. Any question in their minds and they'd just go right up and find out. They'd yank at the beard, or snatch off the glasses, or trip up the bent old guy, and if it was a mistake, they'd say, "Pardon me," and what would the guy with the beard do about it? No. No disguise.

What else?

There was a basement but entrance to the basement was through the rear, and the basement had no connection with any other building. The adjacent building, around the corner and tacked right close to my apartment house, was a hotel, two stories higher than my house, with a large lobby entrance and a small side entrance. But the basement of each edifice were separate. The roof? To get to the roof of my house, one had to ascend a narrow stairway and push open a trap door somewhat like the hatch of a submarine. But this trap door was shut and locked from within. I didn't know a thing about the roof of the hotel but I decided to find out.

A cab dropped me at the side entrance and I slipped in quickly. I took the elevator to the top floor, pretended to stroll the corridor looking for a room number. As soon as the elevator closed, I began a more careful inspection. I came to a door marked: ROOF GARDEN. I opened that, ran up a flight of stairs, pushed open another door, and I was on a dark roof with potted palms, iron tables with umbrellas growing out of their middles, iron chairs around these tables, and lounging chairs of the beach-type variety strewn all over the place. Light rising from the neons of Manhattan provided a dim, fantastic, cloudy illumination. I was on a solarium of sorts. Brick walls rose about four feet on each side. There was a break in the wall on the side touching my apartment house. I went to that quickly. The break opened upon a fire escape which ran down the two stories to my roof. Here was an emergency fire exit. But it explained why the trap door on my roof was always shut and locked: otherwise it would have been too easy for the uninvited bent on mischief to invite themselves.

In case of fire, that trap door could be hacked open quickly enough or it could be opened from within.

The rest was easy. I went back to the lobby, crowded into a phone booth, and dialed the number of the house phone in the lower hall of my apartment house. I waited, nerves twanging. Finally, Louis's voice came on: "Hello?"

"Louis?"

"This is Louis."

"Mr. Chambers, Louis."

"He's got his own phone, upstairs. We don't call no tenants down here. This is for the convenience of the tenants in case—"

"Louis!" I screamed.

Mildly he said, "This is Louis."

"*This* is Mr. Chambers. Here. Peter Chambers. I'm here. Me. Here. I'm talking to you."

"Oh. I didn't see you come in, Mr. Chambers. Fact, I ain't seen you around for a couple nights. Been away?"

"I'm not in, Louis."

"Not in?"

"Out."

"Out?"

"Look, Louis, let's do it nice and slow. Okay, Louis?"

"Anything you say, Mr. Chambers."

"I'm calling you from outside."

"Oh."

"I can't get in."

"Key busted or something? You leave it to Louis."

"It's not that, Louis. There are people waiting for me."

"Well, I'll have them come in. I'll have them wait in the lobby. That's what we got all the nice soft chairs for."

"No, Louis. These are not friends of mine. These are hoodlums. The minute they see me, they start making with the artillery."

"You leave it to Louis." There was excitement in his voice now. "I'll get cops. I'll attend to everything. Just leave it to Louis."

"No," I yelled. "I don't want you to do a thing. Not a thing."

There was a moment of pause, then plaintively, "So what did you call me for . . . if you don't want I should do nothing?"

I wiped sweat from my forehead with the back of my hand. "Louis, we're at cross-purposes. We got tangled up. I *do* want you to do something for me and it's very important."

His voice brightened. "Yes, sir, Mr. Chambers."

"I'm in the hotel next door."

"Yes, sir."

"I'm going up to their roof."

"Yes, sir."

"They've got a fire escape going down to our roof."

"Yes, sir."

"I want you to go upstairs and open up the trap door. The one on our roof. Okay, Louis?"

"Yes, *sir.*"

"Jump to it, Louis. I'll be waiting."

So, in the dark of night, and more than a trifle fretful about somebody who might start screaming or worse, start shooting at a very legitimate individual endeavoring to break into his own apartment—I crept down the iron-rail awkward rattling steps of the fire escape and waited, a lonely figure with bells in his head and birds in his stomach, until the trap door fell back and Louis's head rose up into the night.

"That you, Mr. Chambers?" he whispered.

"Ain't no one else," I said, and practically rammed him down the stairway and scrambled after him.

I waited, fist-clenchingly, until he locked the trap door. I said, "I don't want to use the elevator."

"Figured that. Got the freight elevator up here."

He took me by freight elevator to the rear of my floor. I parted my wallet and fetched up a bill. I said, "Here's for you."

"Thanks. But what's with them hoods?"

"Forget them, Louis. Forget the whole deal." I fetched up another bill and handed it over. "This one's to help you remember to forget."

"Already," he said, "it's forgotten." He smiled, shrugged, closed the elevator door and disappeared.

I put the key in the lock, and I was home. I debated about putting on the lights and I don't know which of me won but I put on the lights. Once more my reasoning was based on the hypothesis that these were not amateurs. If they saw the light and knew it came from my apartment—so what? They were the sentinels. They knew that *I* had not come into the building. I could have sent someone to get something for me—in person. If they felt that somehow I had got by and sneaked in—well, they knew that I was as much a professional in my field as they were in theirs. I wouldn't open the door for them and bow and ask them in to assassinate me. My door would be locked and bolted. (I moved to the door and locked and bolted it).

They might try. They might knock. But then they'd go back to waiting for me to come out.

I went to the bedroom and opened a closet and flung clothes about until I found the odd jacket I had worn when I had first visited Olga Adams in Lido. I dug into the pocket and plucked out the letter that I had jammed away when I'd been whirled around and a man named Paul had pinned my hands behind me and a man named Mike had strutted, grinning in front of me. I flattened the letter and looked at it and the bells in my head simmered down to music.

I was on my way to the phone when the rap came to my door. I didn't answer. Then the door buzzer sounded, loud and long. I wasn't having any. There was another rap, a series, rapid and impatient, and then there was silence. I went to the bedroom, doused the light, and watched through the window. Across the street, on the Park side, a man was pacing. Soon another man joined him. They both looked up toward the lights of my living room. Then they sat down on a park bench and lit cigarettes. I went back to the phone and called Eddie Adams in Lido. I got him, and I said, "Mr. Adams?"

"Yes?"

"Peter Chambers."

"You told me that if I changed my mind, I was to call you. I'd like to come over and see you. I think we've got some business to do."

"Always willing to do business."

"First step is a display of good will."

"Beg pardon?"

"Good will. That's part of business, isn't it?"

"What about good will?"

"Call off your dogs, Mr. Adams. Guy can't talk business with a set of slugs in him. Guy can't talk business if he's dead. Got to have good will, Mr. Adams."

"When will you be here?"

"Within the next couple of hours. Call of your sharpshooters, Mr. Adams. Same story. I've got friends who know I'm coming out to talk with you. Be a real darn shame if I happened to get killed on the way. Trouble. You don't need trouble. Like you told me, you're getting on, Mr. Adams. You want peace and quiet. Let's do it like that, Mr. Adams—peace and quiet."

"I don't know what you're talking about."

"Try. Try hard, Mr. Adams. Think about it. Maybe it'll come to you. Bye, now. I'll be out within the next couple of hours."

I went back to the dark bedroom, sprawled prone on the bed and peered through the window at my two vigilantes on the park bench. I rested, marshalled my thoughts, and watched. Dear Eddie Adams didn't know what I was talking about, but fifteen minutes later a car slid up beside the two men on the bench. A man hurried out of the car, there was a moment of conference and then the three returned to the car, entered and the car pulled away.

I got off the bed, and went out to play target. A live target can quickly be transposed to a dead hero, but I wasn't being much of a hero, I was pretty sure of myself. In the lobby downstairs Louis said, "But . . . but . . . what about them hoods?"

"They're gone."

"You sure?"

"I'm going out to make sure."

I strolled beneath the canopy with all the jumpy assurance of a college freshman being nonchalant while waiting for his first date for the prom. There existed the remote possibility that Adams might be playing potsy—and my body was braced for a bullet. Nothing happened, and I got braver. I lit a cigarette and let the match flare at my face. Nothing happened. My pulse rate was considerably slower as I went to the rear entrance and did a repeat performance. Nothing happened there, either.

I went back, patted Louis's cheek, did a small jig, was whisked upstairs, opened my door and attacked the telephone. Number One was Casey Moore. I told him to come up to my place but pronto. Number Two was Captain Weaver at Headquarters. He was out but I told them it was extremely important, and they said they'd be in touch with him and he'd call back. Number Three was Herb Wiley at home and Herb sounded irritated being called at home.

"What's so important?" he said.

"Two hundred thousand smackers. A testimonial with speeches. Remember me?"

"But I've got company."

"Bring her. Bring a gun too. And bring your car. Pick me up at my apartment. You know the address."

"You kidding about the company?"

"If she likes cops and robbers, I'm not."

"I'll ask her."

"Hurry up, Herb."

My first visitor was Casey Moore. I said, "I think we can wind it up tonight. Here's what I want you to do." I gave him the keys to my car. "Use my car. Go out to

Queens, pick up Simon Gordon and go to Lido. We'll meet at the drug store where we had the ice cream sodas. That's it. Get going."

"But—"

"No time for talk now, Case. Get a move on." The phone was ringing. I hustled Casey to the door, pushed him out, and ran to the phone. "Hello?"

"Chambers? This is Weaver."

"Hi, Captain. It's on that Henry Moore deal. You told me to be in touch if anything popped."

"Yes?"

"It's popped."

"Popped, has it? When and where?"

"Got my tense wrong. It's going to pop. I hope. At Eddie Adams' place. In Lido."

His voice was suddenly nasal. "You sure you know what you're talking about?"

"Fairly sure. I'd like your cooperation."

"What kind of cooperation?"

"I'd like you to get together with the Lido cops. I'd like the Adams place staked out with lots of cops, close but not too close. In about an hour or so, two cars are going to pull up. I'm going to be in one of them, and I'm going to have friends in the other. We're all going in. I've got a hunch there'll be some action. I'd like you guys around."

"You sure you know what you're doing?"

"You know me a long time . . . I generally know which end is up. Will you be there, Captain?"

"We'll see."

He hung up on me. I looked at the receiver, called it names, and flung it back on its bar. I removed my jacket, fitted a shoulder holster over my arm, and packed Casey's Luger into the leather pocket. My door buzzer set up a clamor, and I called, "Okay, okay," and I opened the door for Herb Wiley, alone.

"No company?" I said.

"I didn't ask her. Not when it's your party."

"I don't get it."

"For *my* girls, *I* like to be the hero. I know you. Comes the denouement—any kind of denouement—you're the center of attraction. I'm not bringing my company to admire *you*." Laugh lines deepened around his eyes. "I brought this." He opened his jacket and tapped a beltholster. "Aren't you going to ask me in?"

"Nope." I switched off the lights. "We're cutting out. Now."

We picked up Casey and Simon Gordon and we were

a two-car procession from the drug store at Lido to the pebbled roadway of the Adams' house, ablaze with lights. We got out with a vast slamming of doors, massed at the bottom of the stairs and went up in a bunch. I raised my hand for the knocker but the hugh door was swung open by the wide-smiling Mike.

"Enter, gentlemen. Enter, kindly and welcome."

The door closed and there was the scrape of a heel on the stone floor behind us. We turned to see tall Paul, his little eyes wrinkled like shrunken prunes, his red beefy hand wrapped around the butt of a bulky long-muzzled automatic.

Mike rubbed a finger at the lobe of his pulpy ear. "It's what is called getting the drop, gentlemen. Anybody gets funny, gets ventilated, so don't get funny. Got us a real army calling on the boss tonight. I been told to expect one guy." His finger abandoned his ear and pointed at me. "You, wise guy."

"I brought friends."

"Yeah. So while Paul covers with the roscoe, I do what is called the frisk. Kindly remember Paul is crazy about shooting people. It's a thing in the head."

He did it quickly and he came away with the Luger in one hand and Herb's whistle-clean revolver in the other. He winked at Paul. "As long as they come with artillery this trip . . . hold the roscoe on them. I will go talk to the boss."

He walked off, his heels echoing, to the oak door of the plum-walled room. He knocked and waited and Eddie Adams opened the door. Eddie Adams wore black trousers, tassled black lounging shoes, and a black velvet smoking jacket with satin cuffs and lapels. His throat was covered by a cream-white silk ascot, neatly folded and hooked within the satin of the smoking jacket.

Simon Gordon grabbed my arm and cackled: "That's him."

Adams pointed a finger at Simon. "Who's he?"

"A friend of mine," I said.

"I thought we were going to talk business."

"Real business."

"Was it necessary to bring . . . your board of directors?"

"Real necessary."

Mike said, "They come loaded with hardware. These here." He raised his hands, holding the guns like dumbbells.

"I'll take one of those," Adams said. "The flat one." Mike gave it to him. Adams balanced it in his hand. "Luger. Excellent weapon." He went back to the oak door and pushed it open wide. "All right, gentlemen. Please come in."

We filed into the coral-carpeted room.

Olga Adams was there in a simple, beautifully filled black dress. Her braided gold hair gleamed. She wore no jewelry, no adornments, nothing but the rings on her marriage finger. If there were any bruises on her jaw, they were artfully covered. Adams said, "I believe you know my wife, Mr. Chambers."

"Yes. Yes, I do."

She started for the door. I said, "I'd like it if Mrs. Adams remained here."

Adams smiled. "It's your conference, Mr. Chambers." He made a sign to Mike, who closed the door, remaining on the outside. Olga sat down and crossed her legs. Adams said, "Please remember, Mr. Chambers, that I have two eager sentries beyond that door, both armed, both capable and both exceedingly anxious."

"I've got you topped, Mr. Adams."

"I beg your pardon?"

"I've got cops."

"Cops?"

"You've got two hoodlums parked on the outside of that door. I've got cops by the gross load staked all around the premises."

He was old, all of a sudden. The skin of his face hung loose, the jowls flabby, the flesh wrinkled to pits beneath his eyes. He said, "Cops? Why?"

"Because I'm going to accuse you of murder."

"Murder?" That was Olga Adams. An explosion after a gasp. It was the last sound she made until we were all finished.

"Perfect murder," I said. "Almost. A double-header. And we'll throw in arson, just to round it out."

The tips of the slender fingers of his left hand nervously caressed the smooth muzzle of the Luger. He said, "Suppose we try to conduct this meeting in as orderly a manner as possible. Won't you sit down, please, all of you?"

They sat, all of them except me.

Simon Gordon said, "That's him, all right."

Sharply Adams said, "What's he talking about?"

"We'll come to it," I said.

He turned his back and gracefully he walked a long distance from us to the carved mahogany desk. He turned, sighed softly and sank into the high-backed chair. His elbows came up on the desk and the Luger pointed in our direction. He said, "I'm listening, Mr. Chambers."

"May I introduce my friends?"

"Please do."

"Herbert Langhorn Wiley, an officer of the Coronet Insurance Company. Simon Gordon, delivery clerk of a grocery store in Flushing, Queens. And . . . Casey Moore . . . son of Henry Moore."

The last name brought him up rigid. "Moore?" he said.

"Yeah. Henry Moore's son. Guy was supposed to be dead. Figures. You do a perfect murder, double-header, and a guy comes back from the dead to mess it up. A year later. Perfect murder, Mr. Adams . . . it doesn't happen, not when there's motive, not when it has a basis. You come close, sometimes, real close. Tell you something Mr. Adams, you came the closest I ever heard of."

He was an old man and he was beaten before I started. His face was ashen, the circles beneath his eyes deep and black and quivering. There was a constant, restrained twitching at one corner of his mouth. His voice was toneless and resigned. But there was a dignity about him. This was a strong man and an intelligent one going down and knowing, now, in advance, that there could be no hope of succor. He parried like a boxer unconscious on his feet, but going through the motions. Eddie Adams knew it was over, all of it, but he said, "Speak your piece, Mr. Chambers. Never mind the flourishes."

"Perfect murder." I shook my head. "There's always a loose end. Took a boy who came back from the dead—a year later—to shake it up."

"Speak your piece, Mr. Chambers."

I rubbed one palm against the other as I walked his coral carpet. I said, "You're Eddie Adams. Your Diamond Circle has collapsed. You're a guy with a hundred thousand dollars to his name, cash that is, and you're a guy who's used to a lot more than that. You're in a funk. You're down deep, and you're almost out. And then you pop a proposition to Jack Rawlings, a millionaire and the guy's listening. You want him to back you, and he sounds like he's willing."

"No crime," Eddie Adams said. "No crime in that."

"Only it gets to a point where Rawlings wants you as a partner—with you to invest half. Half means two hundred and fifty thousand dollars, and all you've got is a hundred, and that's dwindling. But you're a fighter, Mr. Adams. Here's a chance to come up swinging—but who's got two hundred and fifty thousand, who's got a quarter of a million bucks?"

"No crime yet, Mr. Chambers."

"No crime's been committed yet. But the groundwork is there, the spur, the reason, the motive. You're Eddie

Adams, a playboy from way back. You're married to an elderly lady and there's a policy for a hundred thousand dollars, double indemnity for accidental death. You play around with that, it tickles in back of your mind, but you're Eddie Adams, you don't fiddle around with planned murder, not when it can kick and blow up in your face. So—just like the devil sent him—a guy comes to you out of left field."

"Who?" Eddie Adams said.

"Henry Moore."

"For what?"

"For fifteen thousand dollars. For a loan."

"How do you know this? How the devil do you know?"

"We'll come to that." I stopped at his desk and hitched up on a corner of it. "Fifteen thousand dollars. A guy crazy in need of fifteen thousand dollars. An old-timer, a man whose only child is dead, a man whose wife is dead, a man alone, no family, a man desperately pleading for fifteen thousand dollars. An idea begins to glimmer in your brain."

His head tilted up. "Idea? Why?"

"Because you remember the guy."

"Henry Moore? I deny that."

"Deny, Mr. Adams. See what good it will do you. You denied it to the police, too." I shifted my position on the desk. "You want me to stop? You want to hear it from me or would you rather hear it from cops?"

"Please go on."

"Henry Moore. A guy you used to know many, many years ago. A guy who was a bank guard when you were a small depositor. A guy who used to trade philosophy with you when you were a little man who ran a little club. Henry Moore. A guy that had a bug on a subject. Euthanasia. You remembered that."

"Remembered what?"

"What he was bugged on. Mercy killing. All of a sudden it began to shoot sparks in your brain. The devil had sent him and you were going to use him. Perfect murder with no kick back. You had it. You had it fine. You had it cold and clear and workable."

"How?" Now he seemed disinterested, a third party fascinated by a story. "How did I have it? What did I have?"

"You had your out. You had your recovery. Had your partnership in what turned out to be the Stardust Room. And you had a guy just desperate enough, just crazy enough, to make it work."

Eddie Adams leaned back against the cushioned brocade

of his chair. He waved his left hand toward the others. He said, "You may be impressing that segment of your audience. You're not impressing me." But Eddie Adams was mouthing words. Eddie Adams didn't mean it. Eddie Adams was a tired old man. But tired or old, curiosity is a prod that pricks even when you're dying. Eddie Adams was dying but he lifted his lips in a grimace that was meant to be a smile. He said, "Go on. I'm sorry I interrupted you."

"You know," I said, "in a cockeyed kind of way, you've got class."

"Thank you. Let's get on with the story."

I moved off the desk and began to walk again. I looked toward Herb, and Herb winked and nodded his head. I said, "From here, I'll do it chronologically. Let's begin with the morning of May 10th. You're in your office, and upstairs walkup. Henry Moore had phoned you and you had told him to come over that morning, May 10th, nine o'clock. You didn't know yet that you could use him. You knew nothing. An old-timer was bothering you. You had your own troubles. You figured on having him over early, getting his story, and giving him a fast brush. Nine o'clock. He shows up. A crazy man presents his problem. He needs fifteen thousand dollars as a loan. You remember him, and all of a sudden the gears shift in your head and you're rolling. You tell him to come back at noon."

His voice was a sick man's exhalation. "Why?"

"Because you needed props. You wanted to get this guy properly squared away."

There was unashamed perplexity on his face. "How do you know this? In the event it were factual—how could you possibly know any of this?"

"Let's skip that. You want me to tell you where you went?"

"I'd like to hear where you *say* I went."

"Dr. Fletcher Lewis."

It threw him. Sweat broke out on his face like a valve had opened and he made choking sounds in his throat. I had him reeling and I kept punching. I said:

"Dr. Fletcher Lewis. You were there at ten-thirty on some kind of trumped-up complaint. He keeps his stationery on his desk. You grabbed a hunk of that, swiped it, and you had what you came for. Back in your office, you wrote out a deal about how your wife was incurably ill and now you had your prop. At noon time, you went to work on Henry Moore."

Herb Wiley stood up. "Frame-job?" he said:

"The weirdest." I talked to Herb now. Eddie Adams was sunk in his chair. The only thing alive about him was the light in his eyes. "He made Henry Moore a proposition. He told Moore he himself was stuck for dough. He gave him the whole *megilla.* Then he told him about his wife, ill, incurably ill, showed him a letter from a specialist which coincided with reports from other doctors: his wife had no more than two months to live. He told Henry Moore about the insurance policy, double indemnity for accidental death. And then he came up with the snapper."

"Snapper?" Herb Wiley said.

"He made Henry Moore this fantastic proposition. He said, in substance: 'Henry, I've got a wife who is dead but not quite dead yet and who is suffering terribly. If she dies by a bullet, in a sense we'd be doing her a favor, plus I'd get two hundred thousand dollars instead of one hundred thousand, and I need that extra money. We're both in a spot, Henry. You can help me, *and* you can have your fifteen thousand free for nothing.' And the desperate man, the crazily desperate man, listened to him."

Herb Wiley said, "What about that prop he had prepared? Did he use it?"

"Of course. Moore wanted some sort of proof, and Adams gave him proof. There's a little guesswork involved here but we've got more than a sufficiency of foursquare facts to fit this guy's behind in the hot seat . . . so I believe I'm entitled to the luxury of a bit of guesswork."

"Entitled, indeed," Herb Wiley said.

"All right, let me give you the picture. Eddie Adams did a deal and did it thoroughly. He arranged to have it look like a burglary up there in Mamaroneck. He wanted Henry to be there at about two in the morning. He'd leave the door open for him. Henry would make a noise, Adams would send his wife out for a look-see, Henry would shoot and leave the premises unhampered. Adams would cover for him and it would be over. A killing during the committing of a burglary. Certainly the insurance company would pay for accidental death on that. Henry Moore would be paid by Adams later on in town. As for Moore, his conscience . . . he had killed a woman who was already dead, a woman who was suffering, he had put a human being out of her misery and Adams' soft palaver was a constant salve."

Said Herb Wiley. "Where did it go wrong?"

"It didn't go wrong. Adams is a fox. He wouldn't leave it wide open like that. He wouldn't put himself in a spot where someone alive could point the finger at him for murder. Not Eddie Adams. So . . . when it was done as he'd wanted it done . . . he appeared with his own heater and he killed the intruder. Big hero and perfect murder. Doubleheader, *and* double indemnity. Two people dead and he's the hero. He had even provided a witness, and an honest witness for the first time in his life—Matt Bennett."

There was no more fight in Eddie Adams. He was an old man, terrified, haggard eyes looking upward, left hand clasped about his mouth to hold back the twitching. "How . . . ? How . . . ?" He talked through his fingers. "Loose end? How . . . ? Please . . . ?"

I thought about taking the Luger away from him. I changed my mind. I said, "A little of it is guesswork, most of it isn't. In your office when you laid it out for him, Henry probably wanted that supposed letter from Dr. Lewis. For himself. For proof if anything went wrong. And you were in no position to argue. You gave it to him, but you had it worked in your mind as to how you'd get it back."

"How . . .?" he said. "How . . . ?"

"You wanted to keep him in line. You sent him home for his gun, and he was to wait there for you, at home; you'd pick him up at five o'clock. You did pick him up at five—and you were seen." I turned to Simon Gordon. "Is this the man that picked up Henry Moore outside his house at 116 Whitehall Place at five o'clock on May 10th a year ago?"

"That's him," Simon said. "That's the man."

"You sure?"

"Absolutely positive."

To Adams I said, "You told the police you'd never known a Henry Moore. We can prove you did. We can prove you picked him up at his home at five that afternoon."

Herb Wiley said, "Then . . . ?"

"Then he delivered him up at that motel in Mamaroneck. Got there at about six o'clock. That put Moore at the scene of the crime. Adams then doubled back to New York. He was worried about the phony letter he had given Moore. It was in his own handwriting, strictly a prop. But he even had that figured down to a tee. He had seen Moore's ramshackle wooden house. *The letter was either there in the house or had remained on Moore's person.* Couldn't be anywhere else. So, at about eleven o'clock that night he was at Whitehall Place, a dead spot in Flushing, Queens. He did a real job there, gasoline, the works. Completely incendiary. As Captain Weaver of the New York Police said, 'Anything that was burnable—burned.' "

"Then?" said Herb Wiley.

"He went home. He got there about one o'clock. He left the door open, and went up to his bedroom. Then the thing played out like he had planned it. After he killed Henry Moore, he looked through his pockets—the one other place the letter could be—and it wasn't there. He was certain it no longer existed."

"Did it," Wiley said, "exist?"

"And how. Loose end, like I told Mr. Adams. Great big loose end. And right now it's looped around his neck and it's going to tighten until it kills him."

Now Wiley was spluttering. "But . . . but . . . he couldn't have been more thorough . . ."

"You can't figure everything," I said. "How was he going to know that Moore wasn't going directly home?"

Eddie Adams straightened in his chair. His glazed eyes twisted toward me. "Didn't . . . go directly home . . . ?"

"No. He went to the Bronx where he changed his clothes. And the letter remained in the clothes that he left up there. I had occasion to see a specimen of your handwriting out here on your terrace, a letter you had sent your wife . . . and when I saw that purported doctor's letter . . . I'm not an expert . . . but there *are* experts to testify about handwriting."

Wearily, Eddie Adams said, "There'll be no need for experts. You're expert enough, Mr. Chambers."

Herbert Langhorn Wiley was suddenly the complete vice-president. He disdained the Luger. He marched up to Adams, pointed a finger, intoned: "Mr. Adams, do you admit that you perpetrated a fraud on the Coronet Insurance Company? Do you so admit before these witnesses? Do you admit that two hundred thousand dollars were paid to you under fraudulent circumstances which together with fifty thousand dollars of your own money, purchased for you an interest in the Stardust Room, presently a going concern?"

Eddie Adams nodded, his head hanging weakly. "I admit all of it, and I congratulate you. I congratulate you, especially, on Mr. Chambers. I had underestimated him. It happens. Sometimes it's meaningless to underestimate an adversary. Sometimes it's fatal. I'm afraid in this case, the latter is true." His mouth was working as he smiled toward me. Then he looked to his wife, looked back to me, wrinkled his nose cutely, half waved the fingers of his left hand, raised the Luger to his temple and pulled the trigger.

Pandemonium burst in all directions. A window was shattered and cops poured in. There was the sound of gunshot in the tomb-like outer lobby, and then the oak door banged open, and Paul was hustled in, bleeding from the neck. Outside, I could see Mike with his hands in the air, pinned at pistol point against a wall. I turned to Casey but he was bent over Simon Gordon who had fainted. Then Olga Adams was near me, sobbing, and I moved with her to a remote corner of the room. Her forehead was against my chest and my arms were around her, as she shook, convulsively. Then her head came up, and her wet eyes clutched at mine.

"Now you know," I said, "what I was pitching for."

"I . . . I . . ." She was whispering. "This is the first time I heard any of it."

"Sure. It was before your time. And even if it weren't, Eddie wouldn't let you in on that kind of stuff. That's not for dolls."

Her eyes stayed on mine. "I . . . I . . . apologize."

"Skip it. For a high-class chiseler, you're going to do pretty good. I happen to know."

"No, no, please don't talk like that, not now, please."

"Okay. One hunk of advice. You're not a bad kid. It's a real world, and it's a pretty tough one. Snap out of it. Maybe today you got a couple of years of experience all clumped together, concentrated. Maybe it'll do you good."

"Yes. Yes, Mr. Chambers. Yes, sir." She was like a little girl, clinging, listening to Papa. I was beginning to enjoy the clinging, so I pushed her off.

"Get yourself a good lawyer, get your assets in order, and blow the whole deal. Simmer down, forget the movies, and stop playing small-time big shot. And about that thing in the Bronx . . . it never happened as far as you're concerned. You're out of it."

"Thank you. Thank you, sir."

"The Stardust Room, that'll probably change a lot of hands now, but if you get a smart lawyer, a big hunk of that will fall into your lap in cash. Take it. Don't try to operate that room. It's not for you. You . . . you're retiring at an early age . . . with plenty of moolah."

"Whatever you say. Thank you. Thank you, sir."

Herb Wiley took her away. Weaver was stooped over Eddie Adams, retrieving the Luger, when I said, "Don't mess with tht Luger, Captain. It figures in another homicide."

He had a fountain pen thrust through the trigger guard and he came up with it. "Another homicide? Whose?"

"Frankie Gold."

His forehead creased as his eyebrows hoisted. He brought the gun to a cop, came back to me, called Herb to us, said, "We gotta talk, fellas."

We talked. For a long time. Then Captain Weaver said, "I'm going to need statements and stuff from you. And don't worry about that Frankie Gold. That certainly was self-defense. In the circumstances, they ought to strike a medal for you."

"Thanks. How about tomorrow?"

"Tomorrow? For what?"

"The statements and stuff."

"Fine. Tomorrow's fine."

Herb said, "I've got to get back to town."

"Me too," I said.

Weaver was talking to Casey Moore. Weaver said, "Would you stick around, kid? I wish you would."

Casey looked toward me. "All right?"

"Sure."

"What about your car?"

"Hang on to it. Call me tomorrow. Herb'll drive me back."

Herb looked about. "Who's coming with me?"

"I'm coming with you," I said.

We used the Triboro driving back to town. It was a beautiful starlit night, cool and brisk. Herb said, "Do you have that doctor's letter. I mean the one that's supposed to be the doctor's letter?"

"I've got everything, Herb."

"I'm going to need all the physical evidence and, like Weaver, I'm going to need statements, from everybody."

"You'll get the works, pal. How's it look?"

"Can't miss. You can be paid tomorrow, if you want it."

"I want it cut up a little, Herb."

"Cut up? How?"

I opened the butterfly window and let the breeze whisk in. I said, "You folks got a branch in Miami?"

"Of course."

"This is what I want you to do, Herb Tomorrow. And it's important."

"You call it, kid."

"You get in touch with your Miami branch. Fifteen thousand dollars of my fee—but not called my fee or anything like that—goes to Mrs. Mary Davis, 90 Blossom Street, City of Miami. Cash, certified check, any way she wants it. Explain it anyway you like. That you've got a standing reward and she earned it. That her information broke the case, that she saved your company two hundred thousand dollars—any explanation that fits. But get that money to her, and get it to her tomorrow. I'll give you all the details of her connection with this thing in the morning." I looked at his profile. "Okay?"

He nodded. "In the bag."

"Thanks, Herb."

"What's it all about?"

"Tell you in the morning."

"How about the balance?"

"That's my end. Five big ones. Pay when you like."

He sneaked a look toward me. "You're a queer one, Pete. Nobody can figure you and I don't even try any more."

"Who," I said, "can figure whom? In the ultimate analysis I mean, who the hell really knows anybody else?"

"Now there's a fit subject for chit-chat. Let's have a go at it. Get our minds off blood and murder."

Chit-chat ended when he dumped me at my apartment house. Louis opened the door for me, said, "How's with hoodlums?"

"Hoodlums?" My gaze was naïve. "Are you kidding?"

Upstairs, I drew a bath. I added real he-man-odor-bath-salts. I lay out, long and luxuriously in a warm and peaceful bath, reading from a book of plays but keeping an eye on the time. I got out, had a cold shower and rubbed down vigorously. I shaved meticulously, attending carefully to every nick. I used my proudest after-shaving lotion. I patted on powder, washed my hands, fiddled with my hair. I donned underwear with initials (a birthday present), black silk socks, fancy black evening pumps, a crisp white pleated evening shirt, black tie, a hand-sewn lightweight tuxedo and, after a hand-to-hand tussle with hat boxes high in a closet, I produced a narrow-brimmed black Homburg that would have done credit to a diplomat at a political funeral. Arrayed in all my finery, and smelling like a svelte salesman for a discreet bordello, I presented myself, at precisely midnight, at 666 Park Avenue, apartment 7A. I laid a languid finger on the buzzer and buzzed.

Jane Rawlings called: "Come in." I'd hardly opened the door when she commanded, "Click that clicker, will you? It locks the door." I pushed the thing in the lock, closed the door behind me, whipped off my Homburg and bowed.

"Me," I declared. "With tuxedo. Finally."

No vision of loveliness rushed up to meet me. Nothing rushed up to meet me. I unbent from my bow and glared fretfully into the living room. Jane Rawlings, figure rapturously glistening in silver lounging pajamas, was stretched supine on the couch, one leg up on the arm-rest. She wore no make-up at all. Her hair was tied in a knot on top of her head. Lugubriously, she wailed, "Well, come in. Don't just stand there."

Stiffly. I moved down the three steps into the living room. "Waldorf," I said. "Charity affair. Ichabod Rally's Party. Life begins at midnight. Me in a tuxedo. What, if you'll pardon the expression, the hell happened?"

"Men." she said.

"Men?" I inquired.

"Men. They think things happen to them. I bet you think you had a rough day."

"Depends." I shrugged as best I could shrug in evening clothes.

"Go get yourself a drink, my sweet-smelling soulmate. Then sit down on the hassock and listen to a short tale of woe."

I scaled the Homburg toward one of the bar stools and it landed on the floor. I went to the bar, made a drink, "I sit and I listen."

She regarded me dourly over lowered lids. "You're far too sweet for words."

"Real good mood, aren't you?" I saluted with raised highball glass.

"Put down the drink and listen. Please."

I put the drink on the floor and folded my hands in my lap. I said, "Still I sit, and still I listen."

"Everything's gone wrong."

"But everything?"

"Remember about the man from Paris?"

"The one with the divine jewelry?"

"That one. He never showed up for his appointment."

"Tough."

"And remember Georgette? Georgette who makes me beautiful? The one and only Georgette?"

"She was mentioned . . ."

"Never showed up. But at least she called. That is, her grandmother called. Laid up with the virus."

"The grandmother?"

"Georgette!"

"Rough."

"And then late, very late, they delivered my evening gown. Guess what?"

"I'm all through guessing today."

"Turned out not to be my evening gown at all. And when I tried to call, the shop was closed. Bad?"

"Could it be worse?"

"It can. I got so excited, I banged down the phone, tripped over the wire, and this is the result." She pointed a long finger at her foot over the arm-rest of the couch. "Sprained ankle. Simply, my dear, and succinctly, every damn thing's gone wrong. So . . . we shall stay right here this evening, and fondly we shall gaze upon one another."

"And me, finally, in a tuxedo. What better attire for fond gazing?"

She smiled for the first time. She said, "Do me a favor."

"My pleasure."

"Stand up, very carefully, and come here, very carefully, and kiss me, very carefully. I've got my fingers crossed that that doesn't go wrong."

I stood up, very carefully.

I went to her, very carefully.

I kissed her, very carefully.

It didn't go wrong.